THE POWER OF UNSHAKABLE FAITH
IN NAVIGATING LIFE'S TRIALS

DR. RINA LUCAS

© **Copyright 2025, DR. RINA LUCAS**

All rights reserved. No portion of this publication may be reproduced, distributed, or transmitted in any form or by any means—including photocopying, recording, or other electronic or mechanical methods—without the prior written consent of the publisher, except for brief quotations used in critical reviews or noncommercial purposes permitted under copyright law.

Cilegnari Publishing Co.
First Printing Edition 2025.

Scripture quotations designated (NKJV) are drawn from the **New King James Version**®. Copyright © 1982 by Thomas Nelson. Used with permission. All rights reserved.

DEDICATION AND ACKNOWLEDGEMENTS

This book, *The Power of Unshakable Faith in Navigating Life's Trials,* is lovingly and humbly dedicated, first and foremost, to the glory of Almighty God, our Lord and Savior Jesus Christ, Yeshua, our Messiah.

Every word within these pages is a testament to His divine wisdom, strength, and grace, without which this work would not have been possible. He is the ultimate source of all inspiration and insight, and it is my fervent prayer that the Holy Spirit will move powerfully in the lives of all who read this book. May it serve as a transformative tool, fortifying their hearts and guiding them to develop a faith that remains steadfast and unyielding, even in the face of life's most formidable trials.

I dedicate this work with profound love and hope to my cherished children, Edrianne Mae and Raven Mathew. You are the lights of my life and the living witnesses to the trials I have faced and the triumphs God has brought forth. It is my deepest desire that, through observing my journey, you will come to know the depth of God's faithfulness and the power of an unshakable faith. May you carry this legacy forward, standing firm in His promises and trusting in His unfailing love as you navigate the unique challenges of your own lives.

I also dedicate this book with deep reverence and love to my beloved father, Pastor Leodegario Ferraro Jr. Your unwavering faithfulness and steadfast trust in God have been a profound inspiration to me. Throughout your life, you have endured some of the toughest trials imaginable, yet I have seen firsthand the mighty hand of God working in and through you. Your unshakable faith, even in the face of adversity, serves as a shining example of what it means to truly walk with God and serve God. Thank you for being a living testimony of His power and grace and for instilling in me the same unyielding trust in His faithfulness.

To all who pick up this book, my prayer is that these pages will serve as a beacon of hope and a testament to the boundless greatness of our God. May it remind you that no matter how daunting the trials of life may seem, faith in Jesus Christ is the key to rising above every challenge, experiencing His peace, and living a life that glorifies Him. Let this work encourage you to stand firm, walk boldly in faith, and leave a lasting legacy of trust in the unfailing promises of our Lord and Savior Jesus Christ.

PREFACE

Life is an unpredictable journey, filled with moments of triumph and joy, but also with trials and uncertainties that test our inner strength. It is in these moments of challenge that we seek a steady foundation—something to anchor us, inspire us, and guide us through turbulent times. *The Power of Unshakable Faith in Navigating Life's Trials* is a profound exploration of how faith can provide that foundation, offering strength and clarity when we need it most.

This book goes beyond abstract ideas, delving deeply into the practical and transformative power of faith. Faith, as explored in these pages, is not confined to religious practices or spiritual doctrines; it is a universal force that fuels perseverance, resilience, and hope. Whether rooted in a higher power, a deep belief in yourself, or the enduring goodness in the world, unshakable faith empowers you to confront life's adversities with courage and determination.

The author draws on personal experiences, timeless wisdom, and insightful reflections to illuminate the path toward cultivating this faith. Through relatable stories and actionable advice, readers are invited to embark on their own journeys of self-discovery and growth. The lessons shared are both profound and practical, encouraging us to see challenges not as insurmountable obstacles but as opportunities for transformation.

What sets this book apart is its ability to resonate with readers from all walks of life. It speaks to those searching for hope amidst hardship, clarity in confusion, or strength in times of doubt. It serves as a reminder that while we may not always have control over what life brings, we do have the power to choose how we respond—with faith, resilience, and unwavering belief in brighter days ahead.

As you turn these pages, prepare to be inspired, challenged, and uplifted and touched by the Holy Spirit. This is more than a book; it is a companion on your journey through life's ups and downs, a testament to the power of believing in something greater than yourself, and a guide to navigating even the most difficult moments with grace and confidence.

It is with great admiration that I present this work to you. May it be a source of encouragement and strength as you face life's trials, reminding you always of the remarkable power of unshakable faith.

With deepest respect and gratitude,

Dr. Rina Lucas

TABLE OF CONTENTS

DEDICATION AND ACKNOWLEDGEMENTS	iii
PREFACE	v
OPENING PRAYER	1
INTRODUCTION THE FOUNDATION OF UNSHAKABLE FAITH	3
CHAPTER ONE THE CALL TO FAITH	13
CHAPTER TWO WEATHERING LIFE'S STORMS	36
CHAPTER THREE TRUSTING GOD WHEN YOU CAN'T SEE THE WAY	62
CHAPTER FOUR OVERCOMING DOUBT AND FEAR WITH UNSHAKABLE FAITH	88
CHAPTER FIVE FAITH THAT MOVES MOUNTAINS	103
CHAPTER SIX FAITH AMIDST SUFFERING	133

CHAPTER SEVEN
THE FRUIT OF UNSHAKABLE FAITH   153

CHAPTER EIGHT
HOW TO CULTIVATE UNSHAKABLE FAITH   167

CHAPTER NINE
LEAVING A LEGACY OF FAITH   182

ABOUT THE AUTHOR
Dr. Rina F. Lucas   231

OPENING PRAYER

Heavenly Father,

We come before You with hearts full of reverence and humility, acknowledging Your sovereignty over all things. You are the source of all wisdom, the giver of every good and perfect gift, and the wellspring of eternal truth. Lord, we are grateful for this moment to draw nearer to You through the words within this book, and we ask for Your divine guidance as we embark on this spiritual journey.

Holy Spirit, we earnestly invite You to dwell within us and fill us with Your presence. As we read, open the eyes of our understanding and let Your truth illuminate every page. May Your light shine into the depths of our hearts, transforming our thoughts and renewing our spirits. Grant us the gift of unshakable faith—a faith that anchors us in the storms of life, dispels fear with unwavering trust, and draws us ever closer to the heart of God.

Lord Jesus, may we experience Your boundless love and matchless power as we immerse ourselves in these words. Let each chapter be infused with the richness of Your grace, the assurance of Your promises, and the comfort of Your presence. Transform our lives through the power of Your truth and let every testimony shared in these pages glorify Your Holy Name.

Father, You declare in Your Word that Your thoughts for us are of peace and not of evil, to give us a future and a hope (**Jeremiah 29:11, NKJV**). Meet each one of the readers in their unique circumstances, speaking to their hearts with the clarity and tenderness only You can provide. May this book serve as a vessel of Your encouragement and hope, inspiring faith that endures and thrives through life's challenges. Let it sow seeds of transformation, cultivating a harvest of righteousness and drawing many closer to Your eternal love.

We dedicate this time to You, trusting in Your perfect will. Let Your Spirit breathe life into every word, and may the truths reveal here echo in the hearts of readers, producing fruit that remains for eternity.

In the mighty and precious name of Jesus Christ, our Savior and Redeemer, we pray. Amen.

INTRODUCTION: THE FOUNDATION OF UNSHAKABLE FAITH

Faith is the cornerstone upon which our Christian journey rests—a foundation upon which our spiritual lives are built. It's a lot more than an abstract concept or an often-heard word within the confines of the church, but rather that lifeline that nurtures and sustains our relationship with God. Faith is our belief in His sure promises, unlimited power, and preeminent sovereignty. It is in going down life's uneven paths—when there is much struggle, tussles of doubt, and other hard times—that faith takes over, guiding us closer to God in an intimate relationship.

Unwavering faith is resilience itself, a beacon that stands firm through trials and uncertainties. It is profound faith that will bring revolution in our life, enabling us to rise above the obstacles and shape our destiny as desired, drawing closer to Christ. Anchored on His eternal promises, unshakeable faith gives us the courage and strength to face life's most challenging moments with hope and confidence.

In this book, we journey into what unshakable faith in Jesus Christ is. We will discuss the way to develop enduring trust in God through seasons of uncertainty, drawing strength from His unchanging promises. More than anything else, we are going to rest securely in the truth that only Jesus gives the needed strength to the assurance of His presence with us.

As you navigate page after page through this book, take some time and reflect upon your personal walk of faith. No matter where you are or what circumstances you may go through, realize always that you can foster a faith that will stand firm and immovable. The trials that come before you, though daunting, offer the avenue to make your faith deeper, firmer, resilient. Let us walk the path of transformation together, trusting in God for lightening our way and leading us through every step.

UNDERSTANDING THE ROLE OF FAITH IN LIFE'S JOURNEY

Faith is the heartbeat of our existence from the very moment we embraced Christ. Serving not only as the foundation upon which our relationship with God is built, faith is the enduring force that carries us through life's soaring highs and even its challenging lows. Faith opens our eyes to see Jesus as our Savior, as so eloquently put in **Ephesians 2:8-9 NKJV**: *"For by grace you have been saved through faith, and that not of yourselves; it is the gift of God, not of works, lest anyone should boast."* Through this gift of faith from above, our relationship with Him grows, enabling us to fathom the depth of His love and grace, which is beyond measure.

The Bible does give an elaborate and eloquent definition of faith in **Hebrews 11:1 NKJV:** *"Now faith is the substance of things hoped for, the evidence of things not seen."* This verse highlights that faith surpasses belief and is actually the assurance of God's promises even when they are not seen. Faith is a sure confidence in what God says is true-a sure confidence in God's work in us being good-even when life does not make sense and is too hard to bear. Undergirded by the Word and character of God, faith guides as a beacon that lights the pathway ahead, enabling the believer to face life's problems courageously, with hope that does not fade.

Faith has the power to transform our perspective, shaping the way we perceive and navigate the world around us. It invites us to let go of the need for immediate understanding and, instead, to place our trust in the divine wisdom of God's plan. In moments of uncertainty, faith steadies our hearts, reminding us that God's love is an unshakable refuge. It brings comfort in times of despair, offering a peace that transcends human comprehension. Even amid life's most chaotic storms, faith serves as our anchor, ensuring we are not swept away by fear or doubt.

Faith is not a static force in our spiritual journey; rather, it is dynamic, changing with each moment we encounter, whether it is loaded with benefits or marked by adversity. Every time we rely on God—whether in times of joy or adversity—we increase our faith, growing our trust in His unwavering supply and perfect timing. We actively nourish this crucial component of our spiritual lives by praying, reflecting, and studying His Word, allowing it to develop and support us during every season.

Finally, faith invites us to enter into the fullness of God's promises. It acts as a link between the present and the eternal, guiding us to live a life full of meaning, hope, and faith in the Creator who keeps the universe together. As we face life's uncertainties, let us remember that faith is more than a gift; it is a transformative force that inspires us to persist, thrive, and experience God's unlimited love.

THE DIFFERENCE BETWEEN TEMPORARY AND STEADFAST FAITH

Faith is not a one-time decision; rather, it is a lifelong journey that evolves with each day. The Bible distinguishes between two sorts of faith: temporary and steadfast. Temporary faith is sometimes swayed by circumstances or emotions, looking strong when things are going well but fading when difficulties arise, or prayers go unanswered. This type of faith seeks quick results, focusing on the here and now rather than trusting in God's eternal promises, which remain strong despite life's uncertainties.

On the contrary, steadfast faith stands upon the character of God and the immovability of His Word. It remains unshakable before adversity, fear, and uncertainty. The two kinds of faith are illustrated by Peter in **Matthew 14:29-31 NKJV**. As Peter came to Jesus on the lake at Jesus's call, he began by walking in faith, yet his eyes beholding the strong wind and the waves, overcome by fear, caused him to falter. In that moment, Jesus reached out his hand and caught him: *"O you of little faith, why did you doubt?"* His confidence slipped when his focus went from the Savior to the storm around him. Unwavering faith, however, keeps the focus on Jesus no matter what happens.

In **2 Corinthians 4:8-9 NKJV,** Apostle Paul brilliantly shows steadfast faith when he pens, *"We are hard-pressed on every side, yet not crushed; we are perplexed, but not in despair; persecuted, but not forsaken; struck down, but not destroyed."* These astonishing comments by Paul show the depth of his perseverance to such a point that, even though he was experiencing huge tribulations, his faith never wavered. His continued faith was not in favorable circumstances or transitory moments of comfort but in his relationship with Christ, which no temporary obstacles could shake.

Bible Stories That Illustrate Unshakable Faith

Throughout Scripture, we find remarkable stories of people whose persistent faith serves as a timeless model for us all. These stories not only demonstrate the great power that faith can bring, but also the many blessings that come from putting our trust in God, even in the midst of uncertainty and adversity. The continuing power of these stories reminds us that, regardless of the difficulties we experience, trust in God can sustain and raise us in ways we cannot comprehend.

Abraham's Faith (Genesis 22:1-18 NKJV)

One of the most unbelievable and heartbreaking trials of faith that Abraham could ever have faced was when God called him to sacrifice his beloved son Isaac, the very son through whom God had promised to establish a great nation. Put before such an overwhelming command, Abraham found himself in the middle of an intense emotional struggle between the love for his son and obedience to the God who had entered into a covenant with him. In the face of such deep turmoil and seeming contradiction of God's promise, Abraham did not hesitate to obey, trusting God's plan even when it appeared incomprehensible.

As Abraham raised the knife to sacrifice, God intervened and provided a ram to replace Isaac. At this moment of crisis, more than the rescue of Isaac took place; rather, it unfolded as a radical expression of faith in God's faithfulness-to His ability to fulfill the promise, which had become an impossible situation in human terms.

Obedience was one side of Abraham's disposition that exhibited unwavering faith, making him not only the father of faith but also a foreshadow of God's sacrifice of His own Son, Jesus, for humanity's redemption. It is from this story that one realizes true faith at times means to trust in God's more excellent plan even when it goes beyond human comprehension.

Daniel in the Lions' Den (Daniel 6:10-23 NKJV)

The faith of Daniel in God was unmistakable, especially when he continued his daily prayers, even in the face of a royal decree that declared such worship punishable by death. His unshakeable devotion was to the point of being cast into a den of hungry lions, yet his trust in God remained strong.

God intervened miraculously, sending an angel to shut the mouths of the lions and sparing the life of Daniel in the demonstration of the deliverance power of God. Such an extraordinary act of deliverance not only showed the ability of God to protect but also influenced King Darius, who proclaimed God's sovereignty throughout the whole kingdom upon such a great event. It's Daniel's story that again brings to the surface the very truth that standing in faith can literally make all the difference between divine protection and a testimony to others of how great God is.

The Woman with the Issue of Blood (Mark 5:25-34 NKJV)

This woman suffered for a continuous period of twelve years with a condition which rendered her weak, not only physically, in the alienation of people from her. She had been treated by many physicians all of whom proved unsuccessful turning her life in extreme poverty. Yet, even against such discouraging odds, she did not let her faith in Jesus' healing powers falter. She felt that if only she could touch the hem of His garment, she would be restored.

Her faith was granted immediate healing; Jesus noticed the strength of belief and tenderly acknowledged her with the words, "Daughter, your faith has made you well. Go in peace and be healed of your affliction." This striking story is a good testimony of how strong faith in Christ may utterly change and renew a person even in the most hopeless desperate situation.

Job's Perseverance (Job 1:1-22; 42:10-17 NKJV)

Job's life is a case of faith that would not be shaken in the face of unspeakable adversity. The loss of his wealth, children, and even his health could not get Job to curse God. Instead, he continued to worship, confident that in the end, God was just. God later restored Job's fortunes, giving him twice as much as what he lost. The story of Job reminds us that faith is not some kind of inoculation against the hardships of life but a guarantee of the ongoing presence of God and of eventual restoration.

Conclusion

Unwavering faith does not come and go; it is more of an assurance in the nature of God, His promises, and a perfect plan He has designed for us. It is a faith that secures us into truth even in the most violent of storms. The stories of Abraham, Daniel, and many others are timelessly teaching us that faith is so much more than belief; it is the force that enables us to be overcomers, to keep moving forward, and to press closer to God. Their stories remind us that God is faithful to His promises and that if we put our trust in Him, He will never abandon us.

Faith is never without challenges or doubts, but rather these are the means by which faith is usually refined. In fact, it is as we pass through life and experience many testing of our faith that, like gold being purified in a hot fire, it is being strengthened. Abraham's sacrifice of Isaac simply showed a faith trusting God's goodness even when His actions could not be comprehended. The faith of Daniel in the lions' den is a demonstration of the same faith, even when confronted by death staring directly at one. These examples challenge us to be steadfast-our feet firmly set on God's Word and His promises as our guide.

In life, faith that will not easily be shaken requires some deliberate actions: daily surrender to God, persistent prayer, and deep immersion in His Word. **Proverbs 3:5-6 NKJV** says, *"Trust in the Lord with all your heart, and lean not on your own understanding; in all your ways acknowledge Him, and He shall direct your paths."* It challenges us to take away from ourselves the meager reliance of our finite wisdom and wholly surrender ourselves to His limitless wisdom and extensive love. This stance of trust gives God the helm to direct every step we take, even if it has many an indistinguishable path forward.

Unwavering faith makes us be at peace and brave enough to deal with the uncertainties thrown at us in life. It reminds us we do not have to face any challenge alone since God is willing to provide His strength and comfort every step of the way. **Psalms 46:1 NKJV** says, *"God is our refuge and strength, a very present help in trouble."* We are assured that if we put our trust in Him, His grace is sufficient for every situation and His power is made perfect in our weakness.

As we work on building a firm faith, may we remember that it is not by our strength, but by God's Spirit, that we are able to endure. Faith grows as fears, doubts, and burdens are surrendered to Him in trust, *"And we know that all things work together for good to those who love God, to those who are called according to his purpose* (**Romans 8:28 NKJV**). It is in trusting God, day after day that we walk in fullness of His peace, joy, and power.

May we shout confidently, *"I will trust in the Lord with all my heart and lean not on my own understanding."*

May this be the mantra of our life that leads us to lead an unwavering faith. May the lifestyles be the challenge that brings others to the Lord and finds themselves changing through faith unshaken.

CHAPTER ONE
THE CALL TO FAITH

Faith is a heavenly gift, not something we can attain by our talents. **Ephesians 2:8-9 NKJV** says, "For by grace you have been saved through faith, and that not of yourselves; it is the gift of God, not of works, lest anyone should boast." This fundamental truth highlights that faith is profoundly established in God's love and the eternal truth of His Word, rather than arising by human effort. It serves as a reminder that our faith and salvation are not the result of our efforts, but rather of God's kindness and love for us.

Faith serves as the gateway to a transformed life in Christ. When we accept Jesus Christ as our ultimate source of strength, we gain access to power far beyond what we could ever build on our own. Our connection with God is based on trust in Christ, yet that trust is both active and dynamic. This trust encourages us to believe in His promises and rely on His capacity to sustain us, especially during times of doubt and uncertainty. Throughout Scripture, we are reminded of God's invitation to have unshakable confidence. This faith is founded on His unchanging character and is continually strengthened by the power of His Word.

THE FOUNDATION OF FAITH

The call to faith is an invitation of a profoundly transformational nature- to believe in the accomplished work of Jesus Christ: to acknowledge Him as the Son of God, who lived a perfect, sinless life, who took upon Himself at the cross the weight of the world's sins and then triumphed over death through His glorious resurrection.

It is in submitting ourselves to Him that we are freed from the chains of fear, doubt, and the ephemeral wars of this life. Faith not only allows us to rest in the knowledge of God's sovereignty and love but also assures us that He is in control of literally everything around our lives for peace during life's uncertainties.

True trust in Christ goes beyond intellectual awareness of His presence; it is a profound, transformational surrender of our entire being to His will. This trust requires us to let go of our plans and ambitions as we accept the truth that His ways are higher and His purposes much greater than anything we could ever imagine.

Through this submission, we allow His love to form and refresh us, guiding us to live in accordance with His perfect design. Faith becomes the lens through which we see the world, allowing us to face life's uncertainties with steadfast trust and deep confidence in His promises.

At its essence, faith is about recognizing Jesus as the ultimate Source of our strength. In moments when we face challenges that seem insurmountable, faith serves as a powerful reminder that we are never alone. Jesus' invitation in **Matthew 11:28-30 NKJV** speaks directly to our hearts: *"Come to Me, all you who labor and are heavy laden, and I will give you rest. Take My yoke upon you and learn from Me, for I am gentle and lowly in heart, and you will find rest for your souls. For My yoke is easy and My burden is light."* These words highlight the profoundly relational nature of faith—a personal bond with the Savior who, with tenderness and compassion, desires to carry our burdens and grant us the peace that transcends all understanding.

Faith is an effective antidote to fear and doubt. In the face of life's uncertainties, which frequently leave us feeling overwhelmed and defenseless, faith serves as our anchor, rooted in God's constant essence. **Isaiah 41:10 NKJV** provides significant reassurance that settles our hearts: *"Fear not, for I am with you; be not dismayed, for I am your God. I will strengthen you, yes I will help you, I will uphold you with My righteous right hand."* Scriptures like this remind us that faith does not ignore the reality of obstacles, but rather empowers us to face them with unflinching courage and unbounded hope.

Belief in Christ has the ability to change how we approach life's obstacles. Rather than succumbing to despair, our faith encourages us to believe in God's plan, even when the complete picture is obscure. The Apostle Paul elegantly describes this reality in **Romans 8:28 NKJV** *"And we know that all things work together for good to those who love God, to those who are called according to His purpose."* This assurance gives us the confidence to face challenges knowing that God is delicately weaving even our struggles into a broader tapestry—one that displays His glory and leads to our ultimate good.

The Bible is filled with powerful examples of individuals who embraced the call to faith and experienced God's transformative power. Abraham, often referred to as the father of faith, trusted in God's promise of a son despite his advanced age. His unwavering belief was counted by him as righteousness, **Genesis 15:6 NKJV**. Similarly, the faith of the woman with the issue of blood, as recounted in **Luke 8:43-48 NKJV,** beautifully illustrates the profound impact of trusting in Jesus. Convinced that merely touching the hem of His garment would bring healing, she was met with the Savior's affirming words: *"Daughter, be of good cheer; your faith has made you well. Go in peace"* **Luke 8:48, NKJV**. Her story, like Abraham's, speaks to the power of faith and the life-changing blessings it brings.

Faith requires an act of the will and deliberateness. It is through prayer that we open a line of communication with God to a deeper intimacy with Him in our lives. And then, of course, the study of His Word brings both wisdom and assurance; for as we read the Scriptures, we see how He has shown Himself faithful time after time. Fellowship with the saints then enables us to grow in faith, encouraging one another and sharing testimonies of what God is doing in our lives.

As we answer the call to faith, our personal growth is ignited. Faith secures us when things in life get volatile and propels us into a purposeful life, full of joy in Christ. It reminds us that our strength does not emanate from an innate ability within us but from Him who has overcome sin and death. Let us journey forward in faith, holding to the truth that Jesus is our foundation, a rock upon which we stand, and a constant source of hope and peace.

FINDING STRENGTH IN JESUS

To nurture solid faith, we must first recognize its ultimate foundation: Jesus Christ. He is the source of all strength, wisdom, and power, and He provides the unshakable support we require. Faith in Christ transcends our abilities and circumstances because He is the One who maintains everything. As Paul declares in **Philippians 4:13 NKJV,** *"I can do all things through Christ who strengthens me,"* reminding us that our actual power comes from Him rather than ourselves.

As fully God, yet fully man, Jesus was aware of man's troubles, and he supplied the strength needed in overcoming the tasks of life. Jesus invites the oppressed and worn out in **Matthew 11:28-30 NKJV**, *"Come to Me, all you who labor and are heavy laden, and I will give you rest. Take My yoke upon you and learn from Me, for I am gentle and lowly in heart, and you will find rest for your souls. For my yoke is easy, and my burden is light."* These words, so full of graciousness and tenderness, assure us that in Him we have not only relief but strength to endure, with the promise that His yoke is easy and the burden that He lays upon us is light.

When we put our trust in Jesus, we discover a strength beyond our comprehension—resilience that enables us to face our darkest fears, withstand life's hardships, and find peace amid the most violent storms. Although Jesus does not promise a life devoid of adversity, He does vow to walk beside us and offer His support in our times of weakness. Through His presence, we can face life's obstacles with unwavering hope and courage.

Furthermore, Jesus' strength becomes complete in our weakness, a fundamental reality brilliantly described by the Apostle Paul in **2 Corinthians 12:9 NKJV** *"And He said to me, "My grace is sufficient for you, for My strength is made perfect in weakness." Therefore, most gladly I will rather boast in my infirmities, that the power of Christ may rest upon me."* This verse reveals a powerful truth: our limitations are not impediments, but rather chances for God's power to be demonstrated in ways we never imagined. When we choose to hand over our troubles to Him, we allow His grace to work abundantly inside us, transforming our weaknesses into conduits for His might.

The strength of Jesus is not only given in times of hardships but upholds us as we journey normally in faith, enabling us to live a life in which we will love others, forgive others, and press on toward righteousness. His Spirit readies and equips us with the calling to which He's called our lives. As **Galatians 2:20 NKJV** says *"I have been crucified with Christ; it is no longer I who live, but Christ lives in me; and the life which I now live in the flesh I live* *by faith in the Son of God, who loved me and gave Himself for me."* So, through Christ, we are ever enabled, changed, and readied to carry out His purpose.

Faith in Jesus changes the way we perceive issues, from perceiving them as insurmountable obstacles to seeing them as opportunities to grow closer to Him. As **James 1:2-4 NKJV** tells us, *"My brethren, count it all joy when you fall into various trials, knowing that the testing of your faith produces patience. But let patience do its perfect work, that you may be perfect and complete, lacking nothing."* Anchoring our faith in Jesus allows us to face adversities with renewed hope and expectation. We can be confident that He is not only polishing but also strengthening our character and faith for the trip ahead.

We cultivate a genuine and intimate relationship with Jesus through heartfelt prayer and Bible study. This unique link enhances our faith's foundation and increases our trust in Him. As we get closer to Him and stay in His presence, we are gently reminded of His promises and fully reassured of His unwavering love. **Psalms 46:1 NKJV**, *"God is our refuge and strength, a very present help in trouble."* This overwhelming assurance empowers us to entirely rely on Him, knowing that He is always around.

In every stage of life, Jesus is our steadfast foundation. His power sustains us in situations of weakness, His wisdom illuminates our path in times of doubt, and His peace calms our hearts in the midst of life's storms. When we place our confidence in Him, we gain not only the strength to persevere, but also the grace to grow, living a life that reflects His love and glory. As we go forward, may we take unfailing strength from the One who maintains all creation and find profound rest in His enduring presence.

TRUSTING THROUGH DOUBTS AND FEARS

Faith is easy to maintain when life is steady and predictable; yet, its true character emerges during times of uncertainty. In those trying times, we are encouraged to put our trust in God's unwavering character and the sturdiness of His promises, even when our circumstances seem to contradict them.

In **Mark 9:23-24 NKJV**, we witness a father desperate for his son's healing. He begs Jesus, saying, *"But if You can do anything, have compassion on us and help us."* Jesus reacts, *"If You can believe, all things are possible to him who believes."* In a moment of brutal honesty, the father shouts out, *"Lord, I believe; help my unbelief!"*. This encounter perfectly depicts the coexistence of faith and skepticism. It teaches us that faith does not necessitate perfection. Even when uncertainty lingers, Jesus greets us with compassion, demonstrating that genuine trust—no matter how small—is sufficient for Him to operate abundantly in our lives.

Isaiah 41:10 offers a timeless assurance: *"Fear not, for I am with you; Be not dismayed, for I am your God. I will strengthen you, yes, I will help you, I will uphold you with my righteous right hand."* This profound promise reassures us that we are never alone, not even in our most fragile moments. It reminds us that God is both our protector and source of strength, equipping us to confront life's challenges with courage and unwavering faith.

When doubt or fear begins to creep into our hearts, the key is to turn to Jesus for strength and guidance. He doesn't chastise us for feeling weak or uncertain; rather, He lovingly invites us to trust Him more deeply. It's in these moments of vulnerability that our faith has the opportunity to flourish. By leaning into His strength, we allow His transformative power to reshape our fears into confidence, renewing our hope and courage in ways only He can provide.

From Genesis to Revelation, examples of people doubted and feared, yet chose to believe. Abraham believed God for a son when the chances of his wife conceiving were against him, and his faith became the foundation of God's covenant with him.

Moses struggled with feelings of inadequacy yet faced his fears and boldly led the Israelites out of Egypt into the plan God had for his life. Similarly, David, hounded on every side by enemies, found his refuge and comfort in the protection of God unshaken.

He then beautifully says in **Psalms 56:3-4 NKJV**, *"Whenever I am afraid, I will trust in You. In God, I will praise His word, in God I have put my trust; I will not fear. What can flesh do to me?"* These words really reflect the deep-seated truth that during those moments of fear, our trusting in God may be the very bedrock of our strength and peace.

Trusting God in the face of uncertainties and fears includes more than just hope; it requires us to actively remind ourselves of His unwavering constancy throughout our lives. Reflecting on His past provision and deliverance increases our trust in His capacity to guide us through our current difficulties and future uncertainty.

According to **Lamentations 3:22-23 NKJV**, *"Through the Lord's mercies we are not consumed, Because His compassions fail not. They are new every morning; Great is your faithfulness."* This text is a powerful reminder that, even in the midst of adversity, God's love and fidelity remain constant, giving us the strength and assurance we need to face each new day.

Faith that overcomes doubt and fear is not something we acquire overnight. It is cultivated over time through a consistent, intimate relationship with God—through prayer, worship, and a deep immersion in His Word. As we grow in understanding His character and promises, our trust in Him expands, enabling us to confront the uncertainties of life with unwavering confidence.

Overcoming doubt and fear requires a conscious choice to place faith above fleeting emotions. It is a deliberate decision to trust in God's goodness and sovereignty, even when our feelings suggest otherwise. When we choose to trust in Him, He takes our doubts and transforms them into a firm, unshakable faith—one that becomes our anchor through every storm. As we lean on Him, He assures us that we are never alone in our struggles, and with each step, our faith grows stronger.

SCRIPTURES THAT STRENGTHEN OUR FAITH

The Bible provides as a foundation for developing a faith that can withstand life's hardships. Within its pages, we are reminded of God's unfailing promises, limitless love, and the strength we experience in His presence, particularly during times of uncertainty. Scripture provides us with encouragement and resilience to help us get through the most difficult circumstances. When doubt or worry threatens to dominate our hearts, the following verses give consolation and inspiration, as well as hope and guidance:

Romans 10:17 NKJV *"So then faith comes by hearing, and hearing by the word of God."* Spending time in God's Word is essential for growing our faith. The more we listen to and reflect on His message, the more our faith is nurtured. Scripture is a living force that transforms how we think and strengthens our trust in God.

Proverbs 3:5-6 NKJV *"Trust in the Lord with all your heart and lean not on your own understanding; in all your ways, acknowledge Him, and He shall direct your paths."* This verse reminds us that during times of uncertainty, our limited understanding can't compare to God's infinite wisdom. By fully trusting in Him and seeking His guidance, we can navigate life's obstacles with assurance.

Isaiah 40:31 NKJV *"But those who wait on the Lord shall renew their strength; they shall mount up with wings like eagles, they shall and not grow weary, they shall walk and not faint."* This passage beautifully illustrates that placing our hope in God results in renewal. His limitless strength becomes our source of endurance, empowering us to rise above challenges and continue moving forward.

Matthew 17:20 NKJV *"Jesus said, "Because of your unbelief; for assuredly, I say to you, if you have faith as a mustard seed, you will say to this mountain, "Move from here to there, and it will move; and nothing will be impossible for you."* When we trust in Jesus, no matter how small our faith may feel, we align ourselves with His power to overcome what seems insurmountable.

Hebrews 11:6 NKJV *"But without faith it is impossible to please Him, for he who comes to God must believe that He is and that He is rewarder of those who diligently seek Him."* This verse highlights the importance of faith in our relationship with God. It reminds us that trusting Him is the key to drawing closer to Him and experiencing His blessings.

Psalm 27:1 NKJV *"The Lord is my light and my salvation—whom shall, I fear? The Lord is the strength of my life—of whom shall I be afraid?"* In moments of fear, this verse reassures us of God's presence and protection. His light dispels darkness, and His strength becomes our refuge.

Jeremiah 29:11 NKJV *"For I know the thoughts that I think toward you, says the Lord, thoughts of peace and not of evil, to give you a future and a hope."*

This promise reminds us that God's plans for our lives are filled with hope and purpose. Even when we can't see the bigger picture, we can trust in His goodness.

Philippians 4:6-7 NKJV *"Be anxious for nothing, but in everything by prayer and supplication, with thanksgiving, let your requests be made known to God; and the peace of God, which surpasses all understanding, will guard your hearts and minds through Christ Jesus."* This passage offers practical guidance for handling anxiety. By bringing our worries to God in prayer, we receive His peace that surpasses human understanding.

John 14:27 NKJV *"Peace I leave with you; my peace I give to you; not as the world gives do I give to you. Let not your heart be troubled, neither let it be afraid."* Jesus' words here remind us that His peace is unlike anything the world can offer. It calms our fears and steadies our hearts in the face of uncertainty.

As we meditate on these Scriptures, our faith is strengthened, and our hearts are encouraged. Each verse serves as a reminder of God's unwavering love, His faithfulness, and His power to sustain us through all circumstances. By grounding ourselves in His Word, we build a faith that endures and shines as a testament to His glory.

Bible Stories That Demonstrate the Power of Faith

The Centurion's Unwavering Faith (Matthew 8:5-13 NKJV)

A Roman centurion approached Jesus, praying for the healing of his servant. With unshakeable faith, he humbly declared, *"Lord, I am not worthy that you should come under my roof. But only speak a word, and my servant will be healed."* Jesus was extremely moved by the centurion's extraordinary faith and immediately healed the servant from a distance.

This story is notable not only because of the centurion's deep faith, but also because he was a non-Jew who recognized and trusted Jesus' heavenly authority. It serves as a striking reminder that true faith transcends cultural and theological divides. It is a gift available to anybody who believes in Christ's limitless power, regardless of background or heritage.

The Blind Man's Act of Faith (John 9:1-12 NKJV)

Jesus performs a miraculous healing on a guy who was born blind. He spits on the ground, makes mud, and gently puts it to the man's eyes. Then He instructs the man to wash in the Pool of Siloam. The blind man obeys without hesitation, and his sight is miraculously restored as a result of Jesus' instructions.

This act of healing serves as a striking reminder that faith is frequently demonstrated via obedience, even when God's methods appear strange or beyond our understanding. Trusting in His wisdom and obeying His instructions, even when we don't fully understand it, opens us up to His transformative work, allowing it to emerge in ways we never dreamed.

The Israelites' Faith at the Red Sea (Exodus 14:10-31 NKJV)

When the Israelites were stuck between Pharaoh's invading army and the impassable Red Sea, fear and doubt overwhelmed them. The situation looked grim. God, however, directed them to continue forward through Moses. It was an absurd demand, yet they obeyed, and the waters miraculously split. They crossed on dry ground and entered safely.

This awe-inspiring moment reminds us that faith frequently necessitates decisive action, even in the face of tremendous obstacles. When we trust God and go forth in faith, He creates a way where there appears to be none. Through His divine involvement, we are guided to deliverance and victory.

A PERSONAL JOURNEY OF FAITH: TRUSTING GOD IN TIMES OF UNCERTAINTY

The COVID-19 pandemic was an unparalleled storm that swept across the globe, forcing numerous people to make decisions that would have a significant influence on their health, safety, and livelihood.

Among these was the thorny issue of whether to acquire the COVID-19 vaccine—a decision that provoked passionate arguments and left many people in emotional misery. This became a highly personal struggle for me, rather than just a public health concern. I was divided between questioning the vaccine's long-term effects and dealing with the limited evidence available at the time.

During this period of uncertainty, I went to God, desperate for His wisdom, peace, and guidance as dread and confusion seemed to grasp the world around me.

I sought clarity and strength in fervent prayer. It was during those quiet times with the Lord when a conviction settled deep into my heart: a conviction to abstain from the vaccine and comply instead with the requirement of my workplace for regular COVID-19 testing. The decision was not an easy one; it was weighed down by emotional turmoil.

I remember calling my principal-my voice shaking, literally threatening to cry. I emptied my fears and, with determination in my voice, stated my decision. I had been raw in my vulnerability, confessing that if the district made vaccination mandatory, I was prepared to resign, trusting fully that God would provide for me. So, I said, and the words of **Hebrews 13:5 NKJV** brought additional conviction to my heart: *"Let your conduct be without covetousness; be content with such things as you have. For He Himself has said, "I will never leave you nor forsake you."* These reassured me of a divine promise that no loss on earth could sever me from God's continual supply.

To my great relief, my principal reassured me that vaccination was not compulsory and that I could continue with weekly testing. At that moment, I felt an overwhelming sense of peace, as though my prayers had been answered directly—a gentle reminder that God was watching over me and clearing a path ahead. Yet, the decision I had made was not without its hurdles. Some people questioned my choice, and whispers of doubt and concern often drifted through the air, reaching my ears.

There were times when their skepticism made me waver, and fear threatened to take hold. But in those moments of uncertainty, I found strength in the words of **2 Timothy 1:7 NKJV**: *"For God has not given us a spirit of fear, but of power and of love and of a sound mind."* This scripture became my anchor, a steadfast reminder that faith demands courage, and courage is the fruit of a spirit firmly grounded in God's promises.

In times of uncertainty, I frequently took solace in the timeless words of **Deuteronomy 31:6 NKJV**: *"Be strong and of good courage, do not fear nor be afraid of them; for the Lord your God, He is the One who goes with you. He will not leave you nor forsake you*." These lines became my haven, a continuous reminder that I wasn't alone on this road. God's constant presence encircled me, solid and immovable, and His Word shone through the darkness of my uncertainty, guiding me step by step.

In March 2020, when I tested positive for COVID-19, I faced an overwhelming challenge. Yet, through His boundless grace, God restored and healed me, reaffirming His steadfast promise to never leave nor forsake me.

As weeks turned into months, information circulated about people who had suffered negative side effects from the vaccine. Although these tales were varied and inconclusive, they provided as a striking reminder of God's constant protection throughout my life. As I focused on **Proverbs 3:5-6 NKJV**, I felt a tremendous sense of gratitude: *"Trust in the Lord with all your heart and lean not on your own understanding; in all your ways acknowledge him, and he shall direct your paths."* At that point, I learned once more that trust does not necessitate complete comprehension. Instead, it encourages constant trust in the One who possesses all insight, even when the way ahead appears uncertain.

The experience taught me a valuable lesson about faith: faith does not necessarily eliminate fear and uncertainty, but rather encourages us to trust God in the midst of them. **Psalms 56:3 NKJV** perfectly captured my experience: *"Whenever I am afraid, I will trust in you."* Surrendering my fears to God revealed His peace, which embraced my uncertainties, and His promises became the source of the certainty I had long sought.

Reflecting on this chapter of my life, I can see how God, in His infinite wisdom, used every tear, every prayer, and every moment of doubt to draw me closer to Him. My heart is filled with an overwhelming sense of gratitude—not only for the outcome but for the entire journey, which has profoundly deepened my reliance on His unwavering love.

To anyone currently walking through a season of doubt or fear, I offer this heartfelt encouragement: hold fast to the powerful words of **Isaiah**

41:10 NKJV: *"Fear not, for I am with you; Be not dismayed, for I am your God. I will strengthen you, yes, I will help you. I will uphold you with my righteous right hand."* Let these words be a beacon of hope, reminding you that you are never alone.

When we choose to trust God, even in the face of life's uncertainties, we open ourselves up to His unwavering power and calm. His plans, always designed with our benefit and His glory in mind, guide us through every adversity. With His faithfulness, He leads us step by step into the riches of His promises, never leaving us alone on our journey.

Conclusion

When we choose to trust God, even in the face of life's uncertainties, we open ourselves to His unwavering power and calm. His plans, which are always designed with our best interests and His glory in mind, guide us through every difficulty. With His faithfulness, He guides us step by step into the riches of His promises, assuring that we are never alone on our path.

When the weight of life's trials feels heavy and insurmountable, faith in Jesus Christ emerges as a steadfast source of support for us. It gives us the strength we need to endure, reminding us that we are never truly alone in our troubles. Jesus stands with us with each step, delivering His unlimited grace and unwavering love. As we embrace this divine reality, our hearts are strengthened, and we begin to see our troubles as significant possibilities for growth and deeper dependence on Him, rather than overwhelming hurdles.

Immersion in God's Word strengthens and deepens our faith. The Scriptures, full of ageless knowledge, serve as a guiding light, illuminating the path ahead and assuring us of His unwavering commitment across generations. We gain strength and inspiration from reading passages that mirror His promises and reflecting on the faith-filled lives of biblical figures. Abraham's unflinching obedience, Daniel's steady courage in the face of danger, and numerous other testimonies remind us that God is faithful to those who trust Him, even in the most uncertain and stressful circumstances. We are encouraged to stand steady in our faith by these stories, knowing that God's promises are always true and His presence never fails.

Faith makes us act, it enables us to progress, and allows us to act with unshakable faith that God's plans, though they may go beyond our full understanding, are perfect. **Proverbs 3:5-6 NKJV** captures this truth so well: *"Trust in the Lord with all your heart and lean not on your own understanding; in all your ways acknowledge Him, and He shall direct your paths."* This invitation to trust changes our perspective, allowing us to approach the future with hope and eagerness, knowing that His knowledge much exceeds ours. This trust makes us strong and prepared to stand before life's uncertainties, since it is sure that God will guide us in the right direction.

Faith is not something that can be static; it thrives on the basis of an active approach towards a relationship with Christ. It is prayer, worship, and thoughtful reflection that help in developing a better relationship with Him and allow His Spirit to work within us. This journey of faith refines our hearts, gradually aligning them with His divine will. It enables us to live in lives which reveal not just His glory but also His love and grace, even while going through the trial.

Faith is a gift from above, ever so precious, to see us through every season. It is light in the darkest valleys and a fountain of joy in times of triumph. Faith beckons us to let our fears and doubts fall into the capable hands of our Creator-to take us through. May we, as we take up this divine invitation, walk bold in the faith He offers, knowing well that His promises can never fail. Having Jesus for a cornerstone, we shall face the unknown with unshakable hope, knowing His plans are good, His timing is perfect, and His love is eternal.

A PRAYER: EMBRACING THE CALL TO FAITH

Gracious Heavenly Father,

I come to You with a heart overflowing with gratitude, acknowledging Your Word as the firm foundation of my faith. You are the beginning and the sustainer of my journey, and I choose to place my trust fully in You.

Lord, as it says in **Hebrews 11:1 NKJV**, *"Now faith is the substance of things hoped for, the evidence of things not seen",* I anchor my hope in You, even when I cannot see the way forward. I stand on Your promises, knowing that You are steadfast and true.

Your Word reminds us in **Romans 10:17 NKJV** that *"faith comes by hearing, and hearing by the word of God."* Father, fill my heart with Your truth every day. Speak to me through Your Word so that my faith may continue to grow and deepen.

Help me, Lord, to embrace the call to walk by faith. Like Abraham, who trusted Your voice and followed Your command without knowing the full plan **Genesis 12:1-4 NKJV**, may I also step out in obedience, confident in Your perfect will.

As **2 Corinthians 5:7 NKJV** declares, *"For we walk by faith, not by sight."* Strengthen me, Father, to move forward with courage, trusting that You are guiding every step I take. When doubt or fear arises, help me to rest in the assurance of **Isaiah 41:10 NKJV**: *"Fear not for I am with you; Be not dismayed, for I am your God. I will strengthen you, yes, I will help you. I will uphold you with my righteous right hand."*

Lord, let my life shine as a testimony of unwavering faith in You. Teach me to trust You as Peter did when he stepped out onto the water at Your call, **Matthew 14:29 NKJV.** Even when the waves rise and the winds blow, may my focus remain on You, the One who commands the seas and stills the storms.

I thank You, Father, for inviting me into a life of faith and purpose. As I walk this journey, I hold tightly to the truth of **Proverbs 3:5-6 NKJV**: *"Trust in the Lord with all your heart and lean not on your own understanding; in all* *your ways acknowledge Him, and He shall direct your paths."* I surrender all to You, Lord, confident in Your strength, guidance, and unfailing love.

In the precious name of Jesus Christ, who is the way, the truth, and the life, I offer this prayer.

Amen.

CHAPTER TWO
WEATHERING LIFE'S STORMS

Storms are frequently encountered on life's journey—unexpected hardships, times of dread, devastating losses, and periods of great uncertainty. These storms, although persistent and overwhelming, may appear to be shaking our very foundation.

These obstacles, however, are not intended to kill us; rather, they have the tremendous ability to shape and refine us. In **John 16:33 NKJV**, Jesus assures us, *"In the world you will have tribulation; but be of good cheer, I have overcome the world."* Through these words, He reminds us that there is hope even in our darkest situations, because He has previously overcome the very storms that threaten to overwhelm us.

Everyone has difficulties at some point in their lives, whether in the form of health problems, financial difficulties, the grief of losing a loved one, strained relationships, or personal failure. These storms can truly test the core of our faith.

However, it is frequently at these trying times that our faith is reinforced and purified, becoming more resilient and profound. Walking through life's hardships with Christ exposes a profound truth: difficulty does not indicate

God's absence or displeasure. It is an invitation to lean into His promises, strengthen our faith, and encounter His unwavering love and limitless power.

The Bible has numerous instances that clearly demonstrate the power of unwavering faith in the face of enormous adversity. Consider Job, who, despite losing everything—money, health, and family—said, *"Though He slay me, yet I will trust in Him. Even so, I will defend my own ways before Him"* **Job 13:15 NKJV**. Even at the most terrible moments, his faith remained unshakeable.

Similarly, the Apostle Paul, who faced repeated beatings, imprisonment, and terrible shipwrecks, boldly declared, *"I can do all things through Christ who strengthens me."* **Philippians 4:13 NKJV**. These stories remind us that faith, when anchored in Christ, gives us the ability to face even the most severe challenges.

These remind us that our faith is not to insulate us from the inevitable obstacles coming our way but to lean on the arm of the only One who controls all obstacles. He who stilled the tempest with, *"Peace, be still"* **Mark 4:39 NKJV** showed that in the midst of chaos His voice could prevail. And we have found that as we learn to trust Him, a calm deepens within, enabling us to hold fast against the stormiest of gusts.

This chapter will explore how life's challenges-these unavoidable storms-play a very important role in our spiritual development. We can discover hope and strength to help us hang in there by examining some biblical stories of faith in the midst of trials, understanding the purpose of trials, and reflecting on how God shapes us through these problems.

IDENTIFYING LIFE'S CHALLENGES AND THE STRUGGLES WE FACE

Life's challenges are as varied as the individuals who encounter them, appearing in countless forms and varying intensities. For some, these struggles are visible and external—a sudden job loss, escalating financial pressure, or the devastating weight of a serious medical diagnosis.

For others, the battle is more internal waged quietly against feelings of doubt, fear, loneliness, or a pervasive sense of inadequacy. Regardless of their nature, one undeniable truth remains: no one is exempt from hardship. Yet, for those who follow Christ, there is solace in the knowledge that we are never left to face these trials alone.

The Bible provides a profound perspective on adversity, offering both encouragement and a clear framework for understanding life's struggles. In **James 1:2-4 NKJV**, the apostle writes, *"My brethren, count it all joy when you fall into various trials, knowing that the testing of your faith produces patience. But let patience have its perfect work, that you may be perfect and complete, lacking nothing."* At first glance, the notion of finding joy in the midst of trials may seem paradoxical—perhaps even unattainable. Yet, this passage unveils a transformative truth: although trials are undeniably painful, they serve a divine purpose.

Challenges are not random happenings; they are chances for growth and transformation. God, in His wisdom, utilizes life's challenges as a purifying process, just as a skillful craftsman purifies gold with fire.

These experiences put our faith to the test, eventually removing our reliance on transient earthly comforts and pushing us closer to God. When we encounter seemingly insurmountable challenges, it is often a divine call to shift our focus from our limited strength to God's boundless might. When we release our burdens to Him, we discover a supernatural strength and calm that will see us through even the darkest valley.

Apostle Paul offers profound insight into the divine perspective on hardship. In **2 Corinthians 12:9-10 NKJV**, he recounts God's message to him: *"My grace is sufficient for you, for My strength is made perfect in weakness."* In response, Paul boldly declares, *"Therefore, I take pleasure in infirmities, in reproaches, in needs, in persecutions, in distresses, for Christ's sake. For when I am weak, then I am strong."*

These powerful words remind us that our limitations are not mere hindrances but rather gateways for God's strength to manifest within us. It is in our most profound vulnerability that His grace shines brightest, transforming what we perceive as weaknesses into opportunities for His divine power to work both in and through us.

Moreover, trials act as a means to align our perspective with God's eternal purposes. In times of difficulty, it is all too easy to fixate on our discomfort or the obstacles that stand before us. Yet, Scripture encourages us to look beyond the immediate and trust in God's sovereign plan.

Romans 8:28 NKJV reassures us, *"And we know that all things work together for good to those who love God, to those who are the called according to His purpose."* Though the full scope of His plan may be beyond our understanding, we can rest in the knowledge that every challenge is part of a greater narrative—one that ultimately leads to our good and His glory.

Adversity instills in us the essential lesson of perseverance. The act of overcoming adversity strengthens our spiritual muscles, equipping us to meet future trials with greater resilience. In **Hebrews 12:1-2 NKJV**, we are encouraged to *"let us run with endurance the race that is set before us, looking unto Jesus, the author and finisher of our faith."* This stunning artwork reminds us that faith is a lifelong marathon requiring both stamina and constant focus. Each hardship we endure acts as a stepping stone, increasing our endurance and moving us closer to the ultimate prize.

Life's challenges have a profound way of deepening our intimacy with God. In times of ease, it's easy to become complacent, relying on our strength and resources, often neglecting the need for divine guidance. However, it is in the trials that we are shaken from this self-reliance, driving us to our knees and into the comforting presence of the One who holds all things together.

Through prayer, worship, and immersion in His Word, we are reminded of His promises, and His unfailing love reassures our hearts. As **Psalms 46:1 NKJV** declares, "*God is our refuge and strength, a very present help in trouble.*" In the midst of chaos and uncertainty, He remains our anchor, steadying us with His unchanging faithfulness, reminding us that no storm is too great for His sovereign hand.

Recognizing life's challenges as chances for growth and transformation can cause a significant shift in our viewpoint. Instead of viewing difficulties as evidence of God's absence, we begin to perceive them as indicators of His purifying process within us.

Much like a sculptor chisel away at rough edges to reveal a masterpiece, God uses difficulties to shape us into the people He always intended for us to be. Each problem we face is a powerful demonstration of His faithfulness—a monument to His limitless power to redeem and restore, even in the midst of our difficulties.

As we go through the storms of life, let us cling to the unwavering truth revealed in **Isaiah 41:10 NKJV**. *"Fear not for I am with you; Be not dismayed, for I am your God. I will strengthen you, yes, I will help you, I will uphold you with my righteous right hand."* With this tremendous promise in our hearts, we are enabled to confront each hardship with courage, knowing that we are never alone, no matter what problems we face. God's presence is always around us, and His plans for our life are always positive and hopeful.

FAITH THROUGH ADVERSITY: LESSONS FROM SCRIPTURE

Jesus Calms the Storm (Matthew 14:22-33 NKJV)

One of the most vivid examples of faith during life's storms is the account of Jesus walking on water and calming the storm. As the disciples sailed across the Sea of Galilee, a fierce storm swept over them, filling them with fear.

In the midst of the chaos, Jesus appeared, walking on the water toward the boat. Peter, in a bold display of faith, stepped out onto the water to meet Him. However, as Peter's focus shifted to the wind and waves, his faith wavered, and he began to sink. Jesus immediately reached out, lifted him up, and said, *"O you of little faith, why did you doubt?"* **Matthew 14:31 NKJV.**

This story serves as a striking reminder that faith does not guarantee a calm sea, but it does assure us of Jesus' unwavering presence in the midst of storms. For Peter and the disciples, the storm became a classroom—a watershed event in which their faith was both tested and strengthened.

By getting out of the boat, Peter saw firsthand the incredible power of trusting Jesus in what appeared to be an impossible scenario. Far from being a threat, the storm provided them with a priceless opportunity to increase their reliance on Jesus, getting closer to His power and guidance.

Job's Faith Amid Loss and Suffering (The Book of Job)

The life of Job offers a powerful example of unwavering faith in the face of unimaginable hardship. Job, described as a righteous man, experienced devastating losses. He lost his wealth, his children, and even his health. His friends questioned his integrity, and his wife urged him to abandon his faith. Yet Job responded with these remarkable words: *"The Lord gave, and the Lord has taken away; Blessed be the name of the Lord"* **Job 1:21 NKJV**.

Job refused to turn away from God despite terrible pain and uncertainty. Despite the fact that the causes of his suffering were unknown, he opted to trust in God's infinite wisdom and sovereignty. In the end, God not only restored Job's fortunes, but also revealed a deeper truth: suffering has the potential to refine our faith, teaching us to trust God more deeply and pulling us closer to Him. Job's unshakable persistence is a strong witness to faith's resilience, even in the face of enormous trials.

Paul's Perseverance Through Trials

(2 Corinthians 11:23-28 NKJV)

The Apostle Paul stands as a profound example of unwavering faith in the face of relentless adversity. In **2 Corinthians 11:23-28 NKJV**, he candidly recounts the hardships he endured—imprisonments, brutal beatings, perilous shipwrecks, hunger, and the emotional weight of shepherding the churches he had so passionately established. These weren't mere inconveniences; they were trials that could have easily broken even the strongest of spirits. Yet, Paul's faith remained resolute, a steady flame that neither storms nor shadows could extinguish.

In **2 Corinthians 4:8-9 NKJV**, Paul offers a glimpse into his indomitable spirit, writing: *"We are hard pressed on every side, yet not crushed; we are perplexed, but not in despair; persecuted, but not forsaken; struck down, but not destroyed."* These words carry the echo of a man who, though bruised and battered, refused to surrender to hopelessness. They remind us that faith doesn't eliminate hardship but transforms it, infusing resilience and hope into the darkest of moments.

Paul understood that his trials were far from meaningless; instead, they were woven into God's greater purpose for his life. He saw his weaknesses not as limitations but as opportunities to encounter the transformative power of God's strength. Reflecting on this revelation, Paul shares a profound promise from God in **2 Corinthians 12:9 NKJV**: *"My grace is sufficient for you, for my strength is made perfect in weakness."* This unwavering faith allowed Paul to reframe his hardships, seeing them not as insurmountable obstacles but as powerful testimonies of God's sustaining grace and boundless power.

These examples remind us that adversity does not signify God's absence. On the contrary, it serves as a divine invitation to trust Him on a deeper level. Whether we're stepping out of the boat like Peter, enduring the pain of loss, or steadfastly persevering through life's trials, faith enables us to discern God's presence. Even in life's most challenging moments, we can see His hand at work, gently guiding us toward His purpose.

WHY TRIALS STRENGTHEN OUR FAITH, NOT WEAKEN IT

It is a natural part of the human experience to question the purpose of suffering, especially when it affects the lives of individuals who sincerely desire to walk closely with God.

In times of pain, it's tempting to wonder why a loving and sovereign God would allow His children to undergo such difficulties. These difficulties often seem like sharp contrasts to His compassion. However, Scripture reveals a deeper reality that changes our perspective: pain is not a sign of God's absence or indifference. Instead, it is an essential part of His divine plan—a sacred process by which He forms our character, strengthens our faith, and brings us closer, more intimately to Him.

Trials often act as a spiritual furnace, purifying and fortifying the believer's faith, much like fire refines and enhances the value of precious metals. The apostle Peter, in **1 Peter 1:6-7 NKJV,** provides profound insight into the purpose of suffering: *"In this you greatly rejoice, though now for a little while, if need be, you have been grieved by trials, that the genuineness of your faith, being much more precious than gold that perishes, though it is tested by fire, may be found to praise, honor and glory at the revelation of Jesus Christ."*

These passages remind us that difficulties are not useless; they are divine tools used by God to polish and validate our faith. God, like a goldsmith patiently purifying gold, utilizes the fire of life's struggles to remove impurities, leaving behind a faith that is durable, real, and unshakable. While the process may be painful, the result is a deeper, more unshakable faith in Him—one that shines brightly and gives glory and praise when Christ is revealed.

Life's difficulties frequently serve as harsh reminders of our human limits, encouraging us to rely on God's strength rather than our own. In periods of comfort and convenience, it is all too simple to rely on our own knowledge, resources, and abilities. However, difficulties have a way of destroying this illusion of self-sufficiency, softly but forcefully driving us to acknowledge our complete reliance on the Creator.

The Apostle Paul beautifully captures this profound truth in **2 Corinthians 12:9-10 NKJV**, where he recounts God's response to his desperate plea for relief from the thorn in his flesh: *"My grace is sufficient for you, for my strength is made perfect in weakness."* Paul's reflection on this divine reassurance is both humbling and empowering as he declares, *"Therefore I take pleasure in infirmities, in reproaches, in needs, in persecutions, in distresses, for Christ's sake. For when I am weak, then I am strong."*

Trials have a powerful way of aligning our priorities with God's eternal perspective. While it is natural for us to seek comfort and achievement in the present, adversity gently (and sometimes forcefully) directs our attention upward. It acts as a reminder that life on earth is transient and that eternal treasures are far more valuable than any temporary gain.

In **James 1:2-4 NKJV**, believers are exhorted to cultivate a joyful attitude when faced with trials—not because the challenges are enjoyable, but because they serve a greater purpose. These adversities, no matter how terrible, instill tenacity in us. Perseverance, like a competent artisan, transforms us into spiritually mature and complete beings who lack nothing of everlasting importance.

Challenges provide great chances to develop our relationship with God, cultivating a sense of intimacy and trust that goes beyond superficial religion. We often experience His presence most strongly in the valleys of life amidst hardships and uncertainty. We may feel self-sufficient during times of peace and prosperity, but it is only during times of adversity that God's presence becomes clear.

Psalms 34:18 NKJV reminds us, *"The Lord is near to those who have a broken heart, and saves such as have a contrite spirit."* These encounters with supernatural consolation and reassurance demonstrate that, even when life appears overwhelming, God remains actively involved, walking alongside us through every challenge.

Adversity does more than build personal faith; it equips us to be able to empathize with and minister to others in meaningful ways.

The trials we experience position us uniquely to extend compassion and support to those facing similar struggles, allowing our pain to be a wellspring of encouragement and hope. Beautifully, the apostle Paul encapsulates it in **2 Corinthians 1:3-4 NKJV,** *"Blessed be the God and the Father of our Lord*

Jesus Christ, the Father of Mercies and God of all comfort, who comforts us in all our tribulation, that we may be able to comfort those who are in any trouble, with the comfort with which we ourselves are comforted by God." We see a certain higher purpose revealed in these struggles regarding receiving comfort ourselves, with the ability also to pass this comfort onto others. Through them, God refines us while at the same time providing opportunities for us to be the tools of His grace in the lives of others.

Trials are, at times, difficult and complex, yet these provide profound opportunities for spiritual growth and sanctification. In many ways, the athlete is strengthened through his persistent and rigorous training, just as believers are spiritually strengthened in the fires of adversity. This is succinctly captured in **Hebrews 12:11 NKJV**, which says, *"Now no chastening seems to be joyful for the present, but painful; nevertheless, afterward it yields the peaceable fruit of righteousness to those who have been trained by it."*

This verse now whispers softly and powerfully that pain in the trial is never for nothing; it's God's tool, purifying and bringing us into the image of His Son. Though difficult, the product is a life that's filled with righteousness and peace and is well worth each painful moment.

Trials are frequently used as a profound backdrop against which God's power and faithfulness are most vividly portrayed. Consider Job's story, a man who experienced unspeakable pain while maintaining his faith in God.

Although Job's afflictions were terrible, they finally revealed God's sovereignty and provided Job with a deeper, more intimate awareness of his Creator. Similarly, when we overcome adversity and emerge with our faith intact, our lives serve as tremendous witnesses to God's sustaining love and unchanging promises.

Trials often teach us profound lessons about trusting God's timing and His greater purposes, even when we struggle to understand them. In **Isaiah 55:8-9 NKJV**, we are reminded of a comforting truth: *"For my thoughts are not your thoughts, nor are your ways My ways," says the Lord. "For as the heavens are higher than the earth, so are my ways are higher than your ways, and my thoughts than your thoughts."*

When faced with adversity, our limited human perspective is certain to fail. We may wonder why things happen as they do. However, even in the midst of uncertainty, we can find comfort in the unwavering truth of God's sovereignty. His plans, while frequently beyond our comprehension, are based on His infinite wisdom and love. **Romans 8:28 NKJV** reminds us that *"And we know that all things work together for good to those who love God, to those who are the called according to His purpose."*

Even when life feels confusing or overwhelming, we can cling to the promise that His plans are not only for our ultimate good but also for His glory. It's in trusting this truth that we find peace, knowing we are held by a God whose ways far exceed anything we could ever imagine.

In conclusion, while trials may appear to be insurmountable obstacles aimed to shake our faith, they are actually divine tools intended to reinforce and perfect it. God draws us closer to Himself through the crucible of suffering, teaching us to rely more profoundly on Him and changing our hearts to coincide with His eternal plans.

These experiences prepare us to be vessels of His unlimited comfort and grace, allowing us to share the same with others. As we face life's obstacles, we become the people God intended—resilient, compassionate, and firm in our faith. Instead of fearing life's hardships, let us see them as precious chances to strengthen our relationship with God, trusting in His perfect design and unending love.

Trials Purify Our Faith

1 Peter 1:6-7 NKJV says, "In this you greatly rejoice, though now for a little while, if need be, you have been grieved by various trials, that the genuineness of your faith, being much more precious than gold that perishes, though it is tested by fire, may be found to praise, honor and glory at the revelation of Jesus Christ." This is quite a powerful word picture comparing refining gold to how our faith is purified through life's tough times.

Just as gold is purified in a furnace, these challenges test our sincerity-just like fire tests the genuineness of gold-and make it more precious and tenacious. These trials are not pleasant but do have a purpose in maturing us into better glorifiers of God and preparing us for greater opportunities to glorify Him.

Trials Cultivate Perseverance

Trials are not meant to ruin us, but rather to strengthen our perseverance. **James 1:3-4 NKJV** reminds us that testing our faith promotes persistence, which leads to spiritual development. While it is simple to trust God when life is smooth, hardships test our faith, and it is in these moments that we learn perseverance and grow in steadfastness.

Trials Teach Us to Rely on God

We often realize how dependent we are on God throughout life's storms. In **2 Corinthians 1:8-9 NKJV**, Paul recalls on a period of extreme pressure: *" ...that we were burdened beyond measure, above the strength, so that we despaired even of life. Yes, we had the sentence of death in ourselves but in God who raises the dead."* Trials pull away our self-reliance and teach us to rely completely on God's strength and grace.

Trials Draw Us Closer to Christ

In **Philippians 3:10 NKJV**, the apostle Paul describes his own suffering, saying, *"That I may know Him and the power of His resurrection, and the fellowship of his sufferings, being conformed to His death."* Trials allow us to share in Christ's sorrows, deepening our knowledge of His sacrifice and love. During adversity, we grow more intimately attached to Jesus, feeling His presence in fresh and profound ways.

In these ways, hardships help to develop our faith. Rather than weakening us, they strengthen our faith in God, develop our personalities, and draw us closer to Christ.

A PERSONAL TESTIMONY OF UNWAVERING FAITH: STEPPING INTO THE UNKNOWN

Life often unfolds as a series of choices, each shaping our journey in ways both big and small. Yet, some decisions carry a weight so profound that they shatter the very foundation of who we are. One of the most harrowing decisions I ever faced was leaving my ex-husband and filing for divorce. It was a choice I never thought I would have to confront, but the looming fear for our safety left me with no alternative.

The life I had carefully constructed—a home that once felt secure, a stable job I had worked so hard to achieve, and the material comforts many people cherish—had transformed into a gilded cage. Deep in my heart, I knew I had to escape, even though the path ahead was shrouded in uncertainty.

Amid the chaos and heartbreak, a still, small voice stirred within me—the unmistakable whisper of the Lord: "Leave this house." The words were simple, yet they cut through me with such piercing clarity that I trembled.

Every fiber of my being wanted to resist, clinging desperately to the fragile sense of security that the familiar walls around me seemed to offer. But deep down, I knew—obedience to God was the only path forward.

With faith that felt as fragile as glass and tears blurring my vision, I gathered what little I could carry. Each step felt like a battle between fear and trust. I picked up my daughter from school, her face alight with the innocence of a child who had no inkling of the journey ahead. Together, we set off into the unknown, guided only by the quiet assurance that the One who called us would also lead us.

As I drove away from the life, I previously held so dear, a familiar line from **Psalms 37:23-24 NKJV** struck a chord in my heart: *"The steps of a good man are ordered by the Lord, and He delights in his way. Though he falls, he shall not be utterly cast down; for the Lord upholds him with His hand."* These words were my constant anchor. They reminded me that, despite the anxiety and uncertainty that hampered my progress, God was orchestrating every step I took, steadying me with His heavenly hand and assuring me that I was never truly alone.

I had no plan, no clear destination, and no network waiting for me in the state I was heading to. All I had was a single address—a school district I hoped could mark the beginning of a new chapter. With nothing but faith in God to guide me, I called my best friend, Elena, to share the news of my sudden and daring decision.

To my surprise, Elena didn't respond with shock or doubt. There were no questions of whether I had thought it through or reminders of the risks I was taking. Instead, her response was filled with warmth and unwavering support. She assured me that she would reach out to her connections in the state and do everything in her power to help me.

True to her word, within just a few hours, Elena called back with a solution. She had reached out to her network and found a place for us to stay. At that moment, her kindness and resourcefulness became a beacon of hope, reassuring me that even in uncertainty, **I wasn't alone.**

In that moment, I saw God's hand at work, intricately weaving provision into the most unexpected places. With a heart full of optimism, I set my GPS to the new address and drove forward, my trust restored, and my mood elevated. At the same time, my employer showed incredible goodwill by allowing me to use my sick leave, which provided the financial stability I sorely needed while looking for a new career. These blessings, while minor at first appearance, served as significant and irrefutable reminders of God's unfailing favor and faithfulness.

The days that followed were steeped in fervent prayer as I poured every worry, need, and uncertainty before the Lord. With each passing moment, I clung to the promise of His faithfulness. Upon arriving, I prayed over every decision and every step, surrendering them to the One who had always provided. I applied to two school districts, placing my trust in God's plan, and soon, both invited me for interviews.

That same day, as I sat before their panels, something extraordinary happened—God flung open doors of opportunity. I received job offers from both districts, and at that moment, His provision became undeniably clear.

My heart overflowed with gratitude as the truth of **Philippians 4:19 NKJV** resounded within me: *"And my God shall supply all your need according to His riches in glory by Christ Jesus."*

God, ever faithful, answered beyond my expectations. Not only did He bless me with a job, but He also provided a safe place to live—a haven of restoration for my soul. Those tangible blessings also renewed my hope and reignited my sense of purpose. His timing was flawless, and His provision overflowed with abundance.

During this season of my life, the words of **Isaiah 41:10 NKJV** became my lifeline: *"Fear not, for I am with you; Be not dismayed, for I am your God. I will strengthen your, yes, I will help you, I will uphold you with my righteous right hand."* These promises were no longer just words on a page—they came alive, anchoring me in peace and reminding me that His strength and presence were my unfailing foundation.

Looking back now, I can't help but marvel at the unmistakable evidence of God's hand guiding me and my daughter through every step of this journey. What initially seemed like an unbearable loss was, in truth, an opportunity for Him to reveal His boundless power and unwavering faithfulness in ways beyond anything I could have envisioned.

Much like the Israelites wandering through the wilderness, where God provided manna and led them toward the promised land, He graciously led us toward a new beginning.

Philippians 4:19 NKJV echoes profoundly within my heart: *"And my God shall supply all your need according to His riches in in glory by Christ Jesus."* This promise became more than just words; it became a living truth, shaping our path and sustaining us through every challenge.

Though I left behind material comforts, I gained something infinitely greater—a faith that is unshakable and a trust in God that can never be taken away. He taught me that His plans are always good, even when they lead us through trials and uncertainties. The fear I felt when I stepped into the unknown has been replaced by the unshakable peace that comes from knowing that God is in control.

To anyone facing a similar trial, I want you to know that you are not alone. Trust in the Lord, even when the way forward feels impossible. His Word promises in **Proverbs 3:5-6 NKJV**: *"Trust in the Lord with all your heart and lean not on your own understanding; in all your ways acknowledge Him and He shall direct your paths."* These words are not just comforting—they are a guarantee of His faithfulness.

My road has been far from easy or painless, but each step was unquestionably important. Throughout it all, I witnessed the tremendous truth that God's grace is more than sufficient, His strength is perfected in my weakness, and His plans are greater than anything I could ever imagine. Today, I stand here as a living example of His steadfast commitment. Whatever obstacles you face, remember that you can entirely trust Him. He will direct your steps, meet your needs, and carry you through your challenges, just as He faithfully did for me.

Conclusion

Life's storms are an inevitable part of the human journey, inescapable yet deeply meaningful. These trials, while often painful and overwhelming, are not mere happenstances. Instead, they serve as pivotal moments that shape our spiritual and personal growth. In the heart of such challenges lies an opportunity—a chance to strengthen our faith, build resilience, and develop a profound dependence on God.

The Bible is rich with stories of individuals who faced tremendous hardships yet emerged transformed, their faith unshaken and often renewed. Their journeys remind us that adversity is not an indication of divine abandonment but rather a powerful tool for refinement.

Like gold tested by fire, our souls are purified and fortified through these experiences, making us more steadfast and unwavering in our walk with God.

Just as gold is refined in the intense heat of fire, our faith is also perfected through the trials of life. The hardships we face act as a crucible, revealing the hidden impurities in our character. Yet, through God's boundless grace, we are offered the chance to confront these weaknesses, grow beyond them, and emerge stronger, more refined individuals. While this process can be painful and deeply challenging, it is essential for our spiritual growth.

It instills in us patience, resilience, and an unwavering trust in God's plan—even when His ways seem mysterious or beyond our comprehension. Every storm we endure, no matter how overwhelming or prolonged, carries a purpose. It is through these very challenges that God molds us, shaping us more closely into the likeness of Christ.

As we journey through the unpredictable and often turbulent waters of life, we can find a profound sense of comfort in the unchanging promise that God is always with us. He never abandons us, even in our darkest moments. Instead, He walks alongside us, offering His unwavering guidance and strength.

While overwhelming and sometimes terrifying, the storms of life are never ours to face alone. These challenges are not meant to break us but to draw us closer to God. They create opportunities for us to lean on Him, trust in His divine wisdom, and experience His unyielding love.

In these moments of struggle and uncertainty, our faith is tested and refined. It is here, in the midst of the storm, that our trust in Him can deepen. Over time, this faith becomes a foundation—unshakable and steadfast—enabling us to stand firm no matter what life brings our way.

Let us, therefore, embrace the storms that come our way—not with fear or resistance, but with the assurance that they serve a greater purpose. These trials are not mere disruptions; they are opportunities for our faith to grow stronger and for our spiritual character to become more resilient. Each challenge offers us the chance to trust more deeply in God's provision, recognizing that every moment, even the difficult ones, is a tool He uses to shape us into the people He intends us to be.

Just as storm clouds eventually part to reveal clear skies, so too will the trials we face give way to a profound, enduring faith in God's unwavering goodness and sovereignty.

Ultimately, it is through these storms that we are not only refined but also drawn closer to God's very heart. And it is in His presence that we find true peace, unshakable strength, and the reassurance that no storm lasts forever.

A PRAYER ON FINDING PEACE AMIDST LIFE'S STORMS

Dear Heavenly Father,

I come before You today, acknowledging You as my stronghold and my refuge, a constant help in moments of trouble **Psalms 46:1 NKJV.** When life's storms threaten to overwhelm me, I declare that You are the One who stills the storms and brings peace to my soul. I place my complete trust in Your unwavering love and power.

Lord, I stand firm on Your promise in **Isaiah 43:2 NKJV,** which reassures me: *"When you pass through the waters, I will be with you; and through the rivers, they shall not overflow you. When you walk through the fire, you shall not be burned, nor shall the flame scorch you."* Thank You, Father, that regardless of how intense the storms may be, You are always by my side, guiding me through every difficulty.

I remember the disciples in the boat, gripped by fear as they faced the storm. But You, Jesus, rebuked the wind and calmed the sea, saying, *"Peace, be still!"* **Mark 4:39 NKJV**. I pray for Your peace to reign in my heart amidst the chaos, trusting that You are the anchor of my soul, secure and unmovable.

Father, I cling to the truth of **Romans 8:28 NKJV**, knowing that *"And we know that all things work together for good to those who love God, to those who are the called according to His purpose."* Even in the midst of struggles, I trust that You are at work, turning every circumstance for my benefit and Your glory.

Help me, Lord, to embrace joy in trials, as Your Word encourages in **James 1:2-4 NKJV**, *"My brethren, count it all joy when you fall into various trials, knowing that the testing of your faith produces patience. But let patience have its perfect work, that you may be perfect and complete, lacking nothing."* Strengthen my faith in every challenge, Father, and let it grow into a steadfast trust that honors You.

I declare, Lord, that I will not fear, for You are with me. I will not be discouraged, for You are my God. You give me strength, You help me, and You hold me with Your righteous hand. You are my rock, my deliverer, and my shield, and in You, I find my security.

Lord, I ask for the unwavering faith of Job, who said, *"Though He slay me, yet will I trust in Him"* **Job 13:15 NKJV**. Let my trust in You remain unshaken, even when I cannot understand Your plan. Teach me to worship You in the storm and to cling to Your promises, knowing You will never leave me or forsake me **Deuteronomy 31:6 NKJV**.

Thank You, Father, for being the calm in my turmoil, the light in my darkness, and the strength in my weakness. I declare that with You, I can endure any storm, knowing Your grace is sufficient and Your power is perfected in my weakness.

In the powerful name of Jesus, who commands the winds and leads me to victory, I pray. Amen.

CHAPTER THREE
TRUSTING GOD WHEN YOU CAN'T SEE THE WAY

There are times in life when the path ahead seems shrouded in darkness. We may find ourselves facing challenges that feel overwhelming or walking through seasons where the future is uncertain. In these moments, it's easy to feel lost, unsure, and even abandoned. We may search for clarity, direction, or some sort of sign to show us the way. But even when we can't see what lies ahead, we can trust that God knows exactly where He is leading us.

As **Proverbs 3:5-6 NKJV** reminds us, "Trust in the Lord with all your heart, and lean not on your own understanding; In all your ways acknowledge Him, and He shall direct your paths."

Unshakable faith isn't about trusting God only when life feels secure, and everything falls into place; it's about leaning into Him even when the path ahead is clouded with uncertainty. It's about understanding that God's perspective is infinitely broader than our own and that He sees the intricate details we cannot. When we choose to place our complete trust in Him—

especially in moments of doubt or confusion—we are affirming our belief in His sovereignty.

Even when life's puzzle pieces seem scattered, and we struggle to make sense of the picture, we can rest assured that God is carefully orchestrating every detail for our good and His ultimate glory. As **Romans 8:28 NKJV** so beautifully reminds us: "And we know that all things work together for good to those who are the called according to His purpose." This profound promise reassures us that, no matter how lost or uncertain we may feel, we are never beyond the reach of His perfect plan.

Life often presents us with unexpected twists and turns, leaving us at moments where the path ahead is completely obscured. It is precisely during these times—when uncertainty surrounds us, when we feel unsettled, or when we are in a state of waiting—that our faith is tested most profoundly. In these moments, we are compelled to ask ourselves a crucial question: **Can we trust God's plan when we are unable to see it? Can we truly believe in His goodness, even when the way forward seems unclear or uncertain?**

As we face these challenges, we are confronted with a choice: to rely on our limited understanding or to surrender control to the One who knows the beginning from the end. Surrendering to God is not merely an act of submission but one that requires profound faith—a faith that trusts not only in His goodness but also in His perfect timing. While it is easy to trust God when the road is clear, the real test of faith arises when we cannot see what lies ahead. **In those moments, will we continue to trust that He is guiding us, even when the next step remains unknown?**

This chapter investigates how we might nurture and strengthen unwavering faith, especially when the path forward appears uncertain. We shall discover that faith in God's plan does not need us to see the big picture all at once; rather, it invites us to take one step at a time, knowing that He will illuminate the way as we go.

We'll also look at how yielding control to God is crucial for living a faith-filled and trusting life. Surrender, on the other hand, does not imply passivity; rather, it acknowledges that God knows the way, even when we cannot see it.

Throughout Scripture, we encounter numerous examples of individuals who trusted God during seasons of uncertainty when the future seemed unclear, and the path ahead was shrouded in mystery. Figures like Abraham, who left his homeland without knowing where he was headed, and Moses, who boldly led the Israelites out of Egypt despite the daunting obstacles they faced, vividly illustrate what it means to trust in God's guidance when the road is hidden. These powerful biblical accounts remind us that God often calls His people to walk by faith, not by sight.

Abraham's story stands out as particularly profound in this context. In Genesis 12, God called him to leave behind everything he knew, stepping into the unknown with the promise that He would make Abraham into a great nation. At that moment, Abraham had no clue where this journey would lead or how it would unfold, but he chose to trust in God's promise. He took that first step of faith, even when the way ahead was unclear.

Similarly, Moses demonstrated unwavering trust when called to lead the Israelites out of Egypt, facing overwhelming challenges at every turn. In both stories, we see that God provided direction only after they stepped out in faith, reminding us that while we may not always see the path ahead, God is always guiding us with a purpose, even when the road is obscured.

When we walk through seasons of uncertainty, it's essential to remember that God's plan is always unfolding, even when we cannot see the details. Trusting God in times of uncertainty is a powerful declaration of faith. It is a declaration that we believe He is faithful, that He will provide, and that His plans for us are always good.

Just as He provided for the Israelites in the wilderness and for Abraham in his journey, He will provide for us. We are not alone on this journey—God is with us every step of the way.

In the pages that follow, we will delve into practical steps for trusting God when the path ahead is unclear. We will explore how to cultivate patience, embrace God's perfect timing, and find peace amid the uncertainties that life throws our way. Whether you're standing at the crossroads of a difficult decision, enduring a season of waiting, or simply grappling with feelings of uncertainty, take comfort in the knowledge that you can trust God to lead you. His boundless wisdom, unwavering love, and immeasurable power are more than sufficient to guide you through even the toughest of trials.

As you navigate through times of doubt, remember this truth: God is already ahead of you, preparing a way where none seems possible. Place your trust in Him with all your heart, and He will make your path straight, illuminating every step of the journey.

HOW UNSHAKABLE FAITH TRUSTS GOD'S PLAN, EVEN IN UNCERTAINTY

Unshakable faith is not rooted in our ability to foresee the outcome or understand the process; it's about trusting God even when the future is uncertain and unclear. It's easy to rely on our faith when everything is visible and straightforward, when the path ahead is illuminated and we feel confident in the direction we're heading. However, the true essence of faith reveals itself when we cannot see the way forward. It is in those uncertain moments that our faith is tested, and we are given an opportunity to choose to trust in God's plan, even when the road ahead seems obscured by fog and doubt.

The Bible teaches us that faith goes beyond simply believing when everything is clear—it is about trusting in the unseen, the unknown, and the unpredictable. **Proverbs 3:5-6 NKJV** offers profound insight into the essence of such faith: "*Trust in the Lord with all your heart and lean not on* *your own understanding; in all your ways acknowledge Him, and He shall direct your paths."*

These verses remind us that unshakable faith is founded on surrendering our desire for control and our need to fully understand every circumstance. When we rely solely on our reasoning, we often find ourselves overwhelmed by the uncertainty that surrounds us. We may attempt to analyze every situation, desperately seeking answers, but true faith calls us to let go of this need and trust in God's perfect wisdom, even when the path ahead is unclear.

Trusting God's plan requires admitting that we don't always have all the answers, which is frequently the most difficult thing to accept. Before proceeding, our natural tendency is to exert control over our circumstances or to demand clarity.

However, when we make the conscious decision to trust, we renounce the illusion of control and place our total trust in the One who holds the future in His hands. In this act of trust, we welcome uncertainty, knowing that God's knowledge and timing greatly outweigh our own.

In **Isaiah 55:8-9 NKJV,** God provides an important reminder of the great difference between His ways and ours: *"For my thoughts are not your thoughts, nor are your ways my ways", says the Lord. For as the heavens are higher than the earth, so are My ways higher than your ways and My thoughts than your thoughts."* This emphasizes an important truth: God's perspective is beyond our comprehension in ways we cannot imagine.

While we may struggle to understand the causes for particular tragedies or the moments of uncertainty we face, we are confident that His purpose is far bigger than we can comprehend. His design is always based on love and meant for our ultimate good.

At times, we may find ourselves struggling to understand why God is guiding us down a specific path or why He permits us to endure particular trials. It is easy to become frustrated when we feel trapped in a season of waiting or when the way forward isn't immediately clear.

However, it is precisely in these moments of uncertainty that God's invitation to trust becomes most profound. Our faith is not meant to be rooted in what we can see or comprehend but in the trust that God, in His infinite wisdom, sees the bigger picture. He is never unaware of where we are nor where we are headed. His timing—though it may differ from our own—is always perfect.

Trusting God amidst uncertainty means surrendering our desire to know every detail. It is about leaning into His character and holding firm to His promises. It's choosing to believe that God is good, even when our circumstances seem bleak, and trusting that His plan far exceeds anything we could ever devise on our own. While we may not always see the full picture, we can rest assured that God's wisdom transcends our understanding, and His ways are always higher than ours.

God's plan often requires us to walk by faith, not by sight. We may not always understand the "why" behind what's happening, but we can trust the

"Who" who is in control. In these times, when we face uncertainty and our path seems unclear, we are reminded that God's wisdom and love far exceed our own. Trusting Him means that we choose to believe He is good, that He is faithful, and that He is always working for our good, even in the moments when we don't have a clear view of the way forward.

This kind of trust doesn't mean we will never face hardship, or that we will always have all the answers. It simply means that, despite the uncertainty, we choose to rest in the truth that God is always with us, guiding our steps, and working behind the scenes to bring about His purposes. In these seasons of the unknown, we can have peace, knowing that God is not only with us but that He is also leading us to a place where His glory will be revealed.

As we trust God's plan, we are invited to surrender control and embrace the journey, even when it feels uncertain. When we let go of our need to know every detail and trust in God's perfect wisdom, we open ourselves up to experiencing His presence in deeper and more powerful ways. His ways are not our ways, and His thoughts are not our thoughts, but they are always good, always wise, and always filled with love for His children. In the midst of uncertainty, we can confidently trust that He will guide us through, bringing us closer to His purpose for our lives.

Let us take comfort in the truth that while we may not see the way, God is already there, preparing the path ahead of us. He is trustworthy, and His plan is always greater than our own.

THE IMPORTANCE OF SURRENDERING CONTROL

One of the most difficult obstacles we face during uncertain times is our basic desire for control. We frequently feel obligated to comprehend every element of what lies ahead, to predict the outcome before it occurs, and to find comfort in our plans. However, correct and unshakable trust is generated not from the comfort of control, but from the act of relinquishing control to God.

Surrender allows us to align with God's perfect will, trusting that He has our destiny in His hands—even when the route ahead of us is unknown. Through this submission, we find serenity, not in our own strength, but in His unwavering presence leading us onward.

In instances of uncertainty, our need to control frequently gets in the way of trusting God's plan. We feel compelled to handle our situations, make our own judgments, and find comfort in what we can comprehend. However, our craving for control can rapidly become an impediment to experiencing the profound peace that comes from trusting in God's authority. Surrendering control is more than just a decision; it is a fundamental act of faith that requires humility, patience, and a willingness to trust that God knows what is best for us, even when the larger picture is unclear.

Jesus provides us with the ultimate example of surrender in the Garden of Gethsemane, as He faced the immense suffering and uncertainty of the cross. In **Luke 22:42 NKJV**, Jesus prays to His Father, saying, *"Father, if it is*

Your will, take this cup away from Me; nevertheless, not My will, but Yours, be done." Here, we witness a deeply human moment where Jesus is overwhelmed by the weight of the coming sacrifice.

He pleads for another way, yet He chooses to surrender His will entirely to God. Despite His anguish, He submits to the Father's plan, trusting that God's will was far greater than His own understanding or desire for a different path.

This act of surrender exemplifies the core of unshakable faith. It is the willingness to release our own plans, desires, and understanding and to place them fully in God's hands. When we surrender control, we acknowledge that God's wisdom, timing, and purposes far exceed our own.

Even in the most challenging and confusing moments, we choose to trust that God is working all things for our good. This act of surrender is not easy, especially when the road ahead seems unclear or fraught with difficulty. Yet, it is in these very moments that our faith is refined and strengthened.

According to **Romans 8:28 NKJV**, *"And we know that all things work together for good to those who are the called according to His purpose."* This verse reminds us that God is neither far away or uninvolved in our lives. He is fully active, working in any situation—whether joyous or painful—to bring about good for people who believe in Him.

Surrendering control to God does not guarantee that life will be easy or that the road ahead will be smooth and free of obstacles. Instead, it is placing our trust in the knowledge that, even when the road is difficult or the result is unknown, God's plan is always for our ultimate good and His glory.

Surrendering control can be incredibly challenging when we feel vulnerable or uncertain about the unknown. The fear of risks and the worry that God's plan might lead us down a path we are unwilling to take often hold us back.

Yet, it is vital to remember that God's purposes are always rooted in His love for us. His plan is not merely good; it is perfect—even when our limited perspective makes it hard to see. When we release our grip on control, we open ourselves to experiencing His peace, trusting that He, not we, is in charge.

The journey of surrendering control can feel like an internal struggle, where doubt and anxiety often arise, causing us to question whether God will truly guide us in the right direction. It is precisely through these struggles that our faith is strengthened. Every time we choose to surrender our will to God, we grow in trust, discovering that He is faithful and that His plan is always worth following. As we continue to release our hold on the future and place our confidence in His hands, we begin to experience the profound freedom that comes from knowing we are never alone on this journey.

Surrendering control is not merely an act; it is a heartfelt statement of worship. It is a confession of our faith in God's sovereignty and His perfect purpose for us. By surrendering, we choose to rely on His unlimited wisdom and unwavering love rather than our own understanding. The more we surrender, the more we discover the depth of God's faithfulness and the serenity that passes comprehension.

In times of uncertainty, when the unknown looms big, let us look to Jesus for the ultimate example of submission and trust. Just as He submitted His will to the Father in the Garden of Gethsemane, we can entrust our lives to God's capable hands, knowing that He will guide, supply, and protect. Surrendering control allows us to accept the bountiful rewards that come from fully trusting in His flawless plan. In this sacred space of surrender, we discover true serenity, for we know that God is always by our side, bringing us down the path He has prepared with love and purpose.

EXAMPLES OF BIBLICAL FIGURES WHO WALKED BY FAITH

The Bible is rich with stories of men and women who demonstrated profound faith, even when the path ahead was shrouded in uncertainty. Their journeys offer timeless lessons on trusting in God's plan, especially when the road ahead is unclear. These individuals walked by faith, overcoming doubt and fear, and their examples continue to inspire us as we navigate our own uncertain circumstances.

Abraham: Faith That Stepped into the Unknown (Genesis 12:1-4, 22:1-18 NKJV)

Abraham is celebrated as the **"father of faith"** because of his unyielding trust in God, even when the path before him was not revealed. In **Genesis**

12:1 NKJV, God called Abraham to leave his homeland and embark on a journey to an unknown land. He was promised a great future, yet he had no idea where he was going. Despite the uncertainty, Abraham obeyed without hesitation. This trust in God's direction, without knowing the final destination, exemplifies what it means to walk by faith.

Abraham's faith was further tested in Genesis 22, when God asked him to sacrifice his son Isaac, the child through whom God's promises were supposed to be fulfilled. This heart-wrenching command seemed to contradict God's earlier promises. Yet, Abraham's faith did not waver. He believed that God's plan was greater than his own understanding. As Abraham prepared to sacrifice Isaac, God intervened, providing a ram as a substitute sacrifice.

Abraham's story reminds us that true faith often requires us to step into the unknown, trusting that God will reveal the next step in His time. His unwavering obedience, despite the uncertainty, is a powerful reminder that God's plans unfold gradually, one step at a time.

Moses: Faith in God's Deliverance (Exodus 14:10-31 NKJV)

Moses is another central figure who exemplified profound faith. Called by God to lead the Israelites out of slavery in Egypt, Moses faced incredible challenges. When the Israelites reached the Red Sea, they were trapped between the advancing Egyptian army and the vast body of water before them. The situation appeared hopeless. In that moment, Moses trusted God's instructions and assured the people in **Exodus 14:13-14 NKJV,** saying, *"Do not be afraid. Stand still, and see the salvation of the Lord, which He will accomplish for you today. For the Egyptians whom you see today, you shall see again no more forever. The Lord will fight for you, and you shall hold your peace."* His faith in God's promise to deliver His people was rewarded when God parted the Red Sea, allowing the Israelites to cross on dry land and escape Pharaoh's army.

Moses' example teaches us that faith is not always about seeing the way clearly ahead. It is about trusting that God will make a way, even when the path seems blocked. When life feels overwhelming and uncertain, we can trust that God will provide a path through the obstacles, just as He did for Moses and the Israelites.

Esther: Trusting in God's Perfect Timing (Esther 4:12-16 NKJV)

Queen Esther's story is a powerful testimony to the importance of trusting God's timing and stepping into our God-given purpose, even when the risks are high. Esther, a Jewish woman who had risen to a position of influence in the Persian Empire, found herself in a perilous situation. Haman, a high-ranking official, had plotted to exterminate all Jews, and Esther's people were at risk.

Her cousin Mordecai urged her to approach the king and plead for the lives of the Jewish people. However, approaching the king without being summoned was forbidden, and Esther knew that doing so could result in her death. Despite the danger, she trusted that God had placed her in the palace *"for such a time as this"* **Esther 4:14 NKJV**. She boldly declared, *"and If I perish, I perish"* **Esther 4:16 NKJV**, stepping forward in faith.

Esther's faith teaches us that sometimes, following God's will requires courage, especially when the outcome is uncertain. Her willingness to act, even at great personal cost, demonstrates that trusting in God's perfect timing can lead to extraordinary outcomes. God honored her faith, using her position to save the Jewish people from destruction.

The Apostle Paul: Faith in God's Plan Even in Prison (Acts 16:25-34 NKJV)

The Apostle Paul's life was filled with hardships, yet his faith never wavered. In Acts 16, Paul and Silas were imprisoned for preaching the gospel, but even in the dark confines of a prison cell, they chose to worship.

At midnight, instead of despairing, they prayed and sang hymns to God. They had no idea what the next moment would bring, but they trusted that God was still at work. Their faith was rewarded when an earthquake shook the prison, breaking their chains and opening the doors. This miraculous event led to the conversion of the jailer and his family, who were saved because of Paul's steadfast trust in God.

Paul's example teaches us that faith is not dependent on our circumstances. Whether we find ourselves in times of ease or suffering, we can trust that God's plan is always unfolding. Paul's unwavering belief in

God's sovereignty, even in prison, reminds us that God can work in and through our darkest moments, turning them into opportunities for His glory.

These stories of Abraham, Moses, Esther, and Paul show us that walking by faith doesn't always require understanding every detail of God's plan. True faith is trusting God's timing, His wisdom, and His ability to guide us even when the road ahead is unclear. These biblical figures encourage us to embrace the uncertainty of life with faith, knowing that God's plan is always for our good and His glory. Their lives remind us that unshakable faith is not about having all the answers but trusting God through every circumstance and believing that He is faithful to fulfill His promises, even when we cannot see the way forward.

A PERSONAL TESTIMONY OF TRUSTING GOD WHEN THE PATH WAS UNCLEAR: FIRST YEAR OF TEACHING IN THE US

In 2008, I arrived in the United States with nothing but a heart full of hope, dreams, and an unwavering desire to teach. I anticipated sharing knowledge, developing significant cultural exchanges, and supporting my own professional development. However, little did I realize that my first year would quickly turn into a tumultuous journey that would test the very foundation of my faith, resilience, and knowledge of God's plan for my life.

From the moment I stepped into the classroom, it became painfully clear that the road ahead would be anything but smooth. The cultural differences were immediately striking, and every interaction—whether it was managing classroom behavior or communicating with my students—felt like a relentless challenge. My lack of familiarity with the American educational system only heightened my feelings of inadequacy, amplifying the tension I already felt. As a foreigner in a new land, the paralyzing fear of making a single misstep haunted me, knowing that one mistake could jeopardize not just my job but my very right to remain in this country.

The challenges grew overwhelming, each day bringing a fresh wave of difficulties. I walked into a classroom filled with disengaged and, at times, unruly students—each day felt like a rollercoaster, where hope was perpetually dashed by crushing disappointment. I found myself returning home in tears, exhausted not just physically but emotionally.

I couldn't help but wonder where I had gone wrong and why it felt as though I had no control over the situation. The sting of failure was sharp, but it reached its peak at the end of the school year when my principal delivered the devastating news that my contract would not be renewed. "Ms. Lucas, you don't know how to teach," she said. Those words pierced deeper than I could have ever imagined, leaving me feeling crushed and questioning my worth. Yet, even in that moment of despair, I chose not to let bitterness take root. I recognized that my struggle wasn't a reflection of my inability but rather a result of a lack of preparation for the storm I had faced.

The fear of being sent back to my home country was paralyzing. I had sacrificed everything to come to the U.S., leaving behind the familiar comforts of home, and now, without a job, I could not even begin to repay the mounting debts that loomed over me like an ominous storm cloud.

Yet, in the midst of my deepest vulnerability, I found myself turning to God. I clung desperately to the promise of **Jeremiah 29:11 NKJV,** which became my lifeline in that dark hour: *"For I know the thoughts that I think toward you, says the Lord, thoughts of peace and not of evil, to give you a future and a hope."* His words ignited a spark of hope within me, reminding me that even in the face of my apparent failure, His plan for my life was still unfolding. In that moment of uncertainty, I made a conscious choice to place my trust in His guidance, knowing that He had a purpose for me far greater than I could comprehend.

Rather than allow fear to paralyze me, I chose to step forward in faith. I attended a job fair, trusting that God would open a door in His perfect timing. As always, He provided. A new opportunity presented itself—one at a school in a low-income neighborhood, facing even greater challenges than my previous position. At first, the weight of the situation felt overwhelming, but this time, I realized my mission was not to dwell on the past; it was to embrace the future with hope.

I released any resentment toward my former principal and chose to view her criticism as a tool for growth. Turning to **Philippians 4:13 NKJV,** *"I can do all things through Christ who strengthens me,"* I allowed His strength to guide me.

As I embarked on this new chapter, I made a steadfast commitment to growth and learning, fully embracing every opportunity that came my way. I eagerly attended each classroom management workshop, enrolled in two master's programs, and, through perseverance and determination, ultimately earned my doctoral degree.

Along this journey, I also sought to deepen my expertise, acquiring certifications in special education and school administration. Yet, none of this was solely the result of my efforts; it was all by God's grace. He provided me with the strength, wisdom, and resilience needed to navigate the challenges before me. With each step I took, I leaned more profoundly on the wisdom of **Proverbs 16:3 NKJV**: *"Commit your works to the Lord, and your thoughts will be established."* And indeed, God's faithfulness was unmistakably evident in every moment, guiding me through each obstacle and blessing me with success.

His instruction gave me the wisdom and confidence to take on the role of the teacher I had always aspired to be. The dread that had kept me from entering the classroom, as well as the doubts about my capacity to lead, vanished. Instead, I discovered a tremendous feeling of purpose in developing my kids' minds and souls, all while understanding that God had been preparing me for this exact moment.

What appeared like an impossible challenge is now a monument to His unwavering devotion and immeasurable grace. The journey, which was previously uncertain and riddled with fear, has become a live testament to the incredible strength that comes from believing in His perfect purpose.

As I stand in a classroom filled with eager learners, I am constantly reminded that the challenges I once faced were not in vain. Through God's grace, I have emerged stronger, wiser, and more prepared to navigate whatever lies ahead. As **Romans 8:28 NKJV** assures us, *"And we know that all things work together for good to those who love God, to those who are the called according to His purpose."* Even when I couldn't see it, God's perfect plan was unfolding in the background.

To those currently experiencing seasons of doubt, fear, or uncertainty, I encourage you to hold tight to this truth: God is always at work in your life. He is transforming your pain into purpose, turning your failures into invaluable lessons, and using your fears as stepping stones for growth. Trust in His plan, and never give up—His purpose for you is far greater than anything you could ever envision.

Today, I give all honor and glory to God for His unwavering presence and guidance in my life. His grace has carried me through the toughest moments, and I will forever remain grateful for the lessons He has taught me and the purpose He has revealed. *"Your Kingdom is an everlasting kingdom, and your dominion endures throughout all generations."* **Psalms 145:13 NKJV.**

Conclusion

One of the most profound and challenging aspects of our journey of faith is learning to trust God when the path ahead is unclear. This journey often requires us to surrender control, relinquish our desire to understand every detail, and place our unwavering trust in God's perfect and all-encompassing plan.

It is, perhaps, in these moments of uncertainty that our faith is tested the most. When the future is veiled in mystery, and the road forward appears blocked or winding, it is easy to feel overwhelmed by doubt or fear.

As we reflect on Scripture, we are reminded of the countless men and women who were called to walk by faith during seasons of obscurity. They did so with unwavering courage and deep conviction, placing their trust not in what they could see but in God's promises and His sovereign will. Take Abraham, for instance, who left the comfort of his home without knowing where he was headed yet followed God's call with obedient faith.

Similarly, the Apostle Paul endured countless hardships yet remained steadfast in his mission, driven by a conviction that transcended the visible struggles he faced. From Abraham to Paul, the Bible is filled with powerful examples of individuals who chose to follow God's leading, even in the face of profound uncertainty.

These stories remind us that walking by faith often requires stepping into the unknown, trusting that God's plan will unfold, even when the way ahead seems unclear.

These stories serve as a timeless reminder that, even in the face of uncertainty, God's plan is always trustworthy and good. Just as He was faithful to those who walked by faith before us, He remains steadfast in guiding us through our seasons of doubt and confusion.

In fact, it is often during these very moments that we are called to deepen our trust and reliance on Him. When we cannot see the whole picture, we are given the opportunity to lean more fully on His wisdom and guidance.

The Bible encourages us, time and time again, to trust in the Lord with all our hearts and to lean not on our understanding, for His ways are higher and better than ours **Proverbs 3:5-6 NKJV**. This trust, however, is not passive; it demands intentionality and action. It requires us to follow God's lead, even when the path ahead is unclear, and to act in obedience to what we know He has called us to do.

When we release control over our lives and place our trust in God's sovereignty, we can be assured that He will never lead us astray. He promises to guide us step by step, even when the way forward is hidden from our sight. This assurance is not based on our circumstances or our ability to understand the future, but on the unchanging nature of God's character.

He is good, and He desires only what is best for His children, even when the journey is difficult or the destination unclear. We are reminded in **Isaiah 55:8-9 NKJV** that God's thoughts and ways are not like ours, and though we may not always understand why things unfold the way they do, we can trust that He is working all things together for our good and His glory. It is in the act of surrender—surrendering our fear, our expectations, and our need for control—that we open ourselves up to the transformative work of God in our lives.

Trusting God on the unseen path requires both patience and perseverance. It asks us to press forward in faith, even when the road ahead is unclear or the outcome uncertain. During such times, we are reminded that our journey is not about finding immediate answers or seeking instant solutions; it is about drawing closer to God and deepening our trust in Him.

Just as the Israelites wandered through the desert for forty years, relying on God's provision, we, too, are often called to wait in faith for a season, knowing that His timing is always perfect. It is in these moments of waiting that our faith is refined, strengthened, and transformed into something enduring.

As we walk through our own seasons of uncertainty, let us take heart in the knowledge that God is with us every step of the way. He sees the end from the beginning, and He has already prepared a way for us, even when we cannot yet see it.

By trusting Him with our lives, even when the path is unclear, we are invited into a deeper relationship with Him, one built on faith, obedience, and a commitment to follow wherever He leads. Just as He was faithful to those who walked before us, He will be faithful to us, guiding us to the future He has promised—a future filled with hope, purpose, and His unending love. In the unseen path, we discover the profound peace that comes from knowing that we are never walking alone, but that God is our constant companion, leading us toward His perfect plan.

A PRAYER OF TRUST: LEANING ON GOD'S GUIDANCE WHEN THE PATH IS UNCLEAR

Heavenly Father,

I come before You today with a heart full of faith, acknowledging Your sovereignty over all things. You are the Almighty, the One who sees beyond what I can comprehend, and the One who holds every situation in Your perfect control. When the path ahead is uncertain and my vision is clouded, I place my complete trust in You, knowing that You are my guide, my provider, and my protector.

Lord, I declare the truth of **Proverbs 3:5-6 NKJV:** *"Trust in the Lord with all your heart and lean not on your own understanding; in all your ways acknowledge Him, and He shall direct your paths."* Even when the way is unclear, I choose to trust You wholeheartedly. I surrender my limited understanding and rely entirely on Your wisdom. I know that You are guiding me toward the future You have prepared for me.

Father, I am reminded by Your Word in **Isaiah 55:8-9 NKJV**, where You declare *"For my thoughts are not your thoughts, nor are your ways my ways", says the Lord. For as the heavens are higher than the earth, so are My ways higher than your ways and My thoughts than your thoughts."* Even when I cannot see or understand the reasons behind Your actions, I trust that Your plan is flawless. Your ways transcend mine, and Your thoughts are always for my good.

In times of uncertainty, I look to the example of Abraham, who trusted You even when he did not know the destination. **Hebrews 11:8 NKJV** tells me, *"By faith, Abraham obeyed when he was called to go out to the place which he would receive as an inheritance and he went out, not knowing where he was going."* Lord, may I follow Abraham's unwavering faith, trusting in You even when the future is veiled in mystery.

I declare the promise of **Psalms 119:105 NKJV**: *"Your word is a lamp for my feet, and a light to my path."* In moments of darkness and confusion, I trust that Your Word will illuminate my steps and show me the way. Though I may not see far ahead, I am confident that Your guidance will provide the wisdom and clarity I need for each step I take.

I also stand firm on the truth of **Psalms 37:23-24 NKJV,** which says, *"The steps of a good man are ordered by the Lord, and He delights in his way.*

Though he fall, he shall not be utterly cast down; for the Lord upholds him with His hand." Even when I falter or feel weak, I know that You will never allow me to fall. You are my refuge and my strength, and You will sustain me with Your mighty hand.

Lord, I hold fast to Your promise in **Jeremiah 29:11 NKJV:** *"For I know the thoughts that I think toward you, says the Lord, thoughts of peace and not of evil, to give you a future and a hope."* When the road ahead is unclear, I rest in the assurance that You have good and perfect plans for my life, plans filled with hope and purpose.

I surrender my fears, doubts, and anxieties into Your hands. I choose to trust in Your perfect timing and your divine guidance. I know You are with me, and that You will never leave me nor forsake me **Deuteronomy 31:6 NKJV.** Your presence is constant, and I find peace knowing that You Walk with me through every moment of uncertainty.

Thank You, Lord, for being my Shepherd, my Protector, and my Guide. As I navigate through the unknown, I trust that You are leading me to a place of peace, to green pastures and still waters **Psalm 23:1-2 NKJV**. You will provide all that I need, and You will direct my steps in accordance with Your perfect will.

In the name of Jesus Christ, the Way, the Truth, and the Life, I pray. *Amen.*

CHAPTER FOUR
OVERCOMING DOUBT AND FEAR WITH UNSHAKABLE FAITH

Doubt and fear are among the most formidable challenges to steady and strong faith. These feelings frequently take root in our hearts and brains, especially when we face life's challenges, uncertainties, or difficult circumstances. Doubt and fear, like darkness that obscures the light, can distort our sense of God's promises, leaving us feeling uncertain and frightened.

In a world full of pessimism, distrust, and discouragement, these emotions can easily overpower us. Faith, on the other hand, encourages us to put our trust in the unseen and to confidently go into the unknown. Doubt, on the other hand, undermines our faith in God's faithfulness, while terror holds us hostage, causing hesitancy and unease.

In times of struggle, the weight of uncertainty and anxiety can feel almost insurmountable, growing stronger with each passing day. These emotions frequently prompt disturbing thoughts such as, "Is God truly with me in this?" or "Can I genuinely trust God's plan for my life?" In such circumstances, doubt questions the veracity of God's promises, while terror increases our doubts, making the road ahead appear far too dangerous to travel. The load becomes tremendous, calling into question not only the reality of God's plan, but also His very presence in our lives.

Unwavering trust gives us the courage to overcome uncertainty and fear. Faith does not pretend that these feelings do not exist; rather, it encourages us to confront them openly and immediately. True faith draws our attention away from the unpredictable tides of life and toward the unchanging reality of God's Word. When we put our trust in His promises, we find ourselves standing firm—not because we are fearless, but because we are certain that God will be faithful even when everything else around us appears uncertain.

In this chapter, we will delve into the transformative power of unshakable faith, exploring how it equips us to overcome the formidable forces of doubt and fear. Faith, when fully embraced, empowers us not only to confront our doubts but also to challenge the deceptive lies that often infiltrate our minds. It redirects our focus from the fleeting anxieties of this world to the unwavering security found in God's eternal truth.

Through powerful biblical examples and heartfelt personal testimonies, we will witness how others have triumphed over fear and doubt by placing their trust in the unfailing promises of God. By anchoring ourselves in the steadfast nature of His word, we, too, can stand firm, confronting and overcoming the doubts and fears that threaten to shake our confidence in His goodness.

CONFRONTING DOUBTS AND HOW TO OVERCOME THEM

Doubt is an inherent part of the human experience, particularly when we face the unknown or when circumstances seem beyond our control. It often emerges in moments of uncertainty, when the weight of life's challenges makes it difficult to see a way forward. During these times, we may find ourselves asking, "Why is this happening to me?" or "Can I truly trust that God is with me in this trial?" Such questions are natural, and having moments of doubt is not inherently sinful.

However, if we allow those doubts to linger without addressing them, they can begin to erode our faith, creating distance between us and the God who is always present, even in our struggles. Thus, it is crucial to confront our doubts—acknowledge them honestly—and make a conscious decision not to let them undermine our trust in God's goodness and His faithfulness.

One of the most compelling examples of confronting doubt is found in **Mark 9:24 NKJV,** where a father, overwhelmed by desperation, approaches Jesus, seeking healing for his son who an evil spirit has tormented. When Jesus asks the father, *"If you can believe, all things are possible to him who believes.".* The father's response is both raw and honest: *"Lord, I believe; help my unbelief!"*

This moment is profoundly powerful because it illustrates that, even in the presence of doubt, we can come before God with an open heart, acknowledging our uncertainties and asking for His help.

Rather than denying his doubt, the father openly admits it, humbly requesting that Jesus strengthen his faith. Despite his imperfect belief, Jesus responds with compassion, offering both healing and grace. This act of divine mercy reveals that the sincerity of our faith, no matter how small, has the potential to invite God's transformative power into our lives.

When we face our own doubts, one of the most effective ways to combat them is by grounding ourselves in the Word of God. **Romans 10:17 NKJV** reminds us, *"So then faith comes by hearing, and hearing by the word of God."* In moments of doubt, we must immerse ourselves in the truth of Scripture.

The more we internalize God's promises through His Word, the more our faith will grow and be strengthened. Regular engagement with the Bible—whether through reading, meditating on, or proclaiming it aloud—helps to fortify us against the influence of doubt and reminds us of God's unwavering faithfulness to His people.

James 1:5-6 NKJV offers additional encouragement for those wrestling with doubt: *"If any of you lacks wisdom, let him ask of God, who gives to all liberally and without reproach, and it will be given to him. But let him ask in faith, with no doubting, for he who doubts is like a wave of the sea driven and tossed by the wind."* This passage encourages us to seek God for wisdom during times of uncertainty and to trust that He will provide the guidance we need.

Even when doubt arises, we can pray for God to help us overcome it. His generosity in providing wisdom is not limited by our struggles with doubt. Rather, these moments of uncertainty provide an opportunity for God to deepen our trust in His perfect guidance.

THE POWER OF PRAYER IN BUILDING FAITH

Prayer is one of the most potent tools available to believers for overcoming doubt and fear. It is in prayer that we draw closer to God, offer Him our burdens, and align our hearts with His will. Prayer is not just about requesting God's help; it is also a process of surrendering our anxieties, relinquishing our fears, and allowing God to renew and strengthen our faith.

In **Philippians 4:6-7 NKJV,** the apostle Paul writes, *"Be anxious for nothing, but in everything by prayer and supplication, with thanksgiving, let your requests be made known to God; and the peace of God, which surpasses understanding, will guard your hearts and minds through Christ Jesus."* This passage illustrates that prayer is a pathway to peace.

When we bring our doubts, fears, and worries to God, He replaces them with His peace—a peace that transcends human understanding and guards our hearts from the turmoil that doubt can cause. Prayer, then, becomes an avenue for peace, as it allows us to cast our anxieties upon God and trust that He will provide clarity, comfort, and strength.

In **Luke 11:9-13 NKJV**, Jesus passionately encourages us to keep praying, telling us to ask, seek, and knock with the certainty that our loving Father wants to bless us with good things. Even when uncertainty and dread threaten, we are reminded to approach God with confidence, knowing that He hears our prayers and will react in ways that are consistent with His perfect plan.

Prayer is much more than just an act of petition; it is also a profound reminder of God's everlasting presence in our lives, as well as a powerful means of strengthening our faith. Our relationship to God gets stronger in these times of constant prayer, as does our trust in His timing and wisdom.

One of the clearest examples of the power of prayer is seen in the Garden of Gethsemane, where Jesus faces His most intense emotional and spiritual trial before His crucifixion. In **Mark 14:36 NKJV,** He prays, *"Abba, Father, all things are possible for You. Take this cup away from me; nevertheless, not what I will, but what you will."* In this deeply sorrowful moment, Jesus chooses to surrender His will to the Father, trusting that even in the midst of immense suffering, God's plan is perfect.

Through His prayer, Jesus finds the strength to face the impending trial and the courage to follow through with the Father's will. This profound moment teaches us that prayer does not always take away our fear or remove the source of our doubt, but it does equip us with the strength to persevere and trust in God's plan.

JESUS AS THE ULTIMATE EXAMPLE OF FAITH IN GOD'S PROMISES

Jesus Christ stands as the supreme example of how to overcome doubt and fear with unwavering faith. His life and ministry consistently demonstrated complete trust in God's will, even when the path before Him seemed uncertain or fraught with suffering. Through His example, we learn that faith is not the absence of doubt, but the ability to trust in God's promises, regardless of the circumstances.

The Temptation in the Wilderness (Matthew 4:1-11 NKJV)

After His baptism, Jesus was led by the Holy Spirit into the wilderness, where He faced a series of temptations from Satan. During this time of intense physical and emotional deprivation, Satan sought to plant seeds of doubt in Jesus' mind, tempting Him to question God's provision and His mission. Each time, Jesus responded by quoting Scripture, reaffirming His trust in God's Word.

Despite the harsh conditions and the temptation to doubt His identity and purpose, Jesus remained steadfast in His faith. His example teaches us that when we face doubts, we too can stand firm by declaring the truth of God's Word, using Scripture as a shield against the lies of the enemy.

The Prayer in Gethsemane (Matthew 26:36-46 NKJV)

As Jesus neared His crucifixion, He experienced deep emotional turmoil in the Garden of Gethsemane. In His prayer, He expressed His desire for the cup of suffering to pass from Him, yet ultimately submitted to the Father's will, saying, *"Not what I will, but what you will."* This poignant moment reveals that even Jesus, in His humanity, experienced fear and distress.

However, His ultimate trust in God's perfect plan enabled Him to surrender His will and find the strength to face the suffering ahead. His prayer exemplifies how we are to approach God in our moments of fear and doubt, choosing to trust in His promises even when the path is unclear or painful.

Jesus on the Cross (Matthew 27:45-50 NKJV)

During His crucifixion, Jesus endured not only excruciating physical pain but also spiritual anguish. In His final moments, He cried out, *"My God, My God, why have you forsaken me?"* While some may interpret this cry as a sign of doubt, it is important to understand that Jesus was not expressing disbelief in God's plan.

Instead, His cry was a reflection of the depth of His suffering as He bore the weight of humanity's sin. Even in this moment of profound agony, Jesus continued to trust in the Father's will. His crucifixion fulfilled God's redemptive plan, and His resurrection demonstrated that even in the darkest of moments, God's promises remain steadfast and true.

Through Jesus' example, we are reminded that faith does not require the absence of doubt or fear, but the courage to trust in God's promises, even in the most challenging circumstances. In moments of doubt, we can follow Jesus' lead—grounding ourselves in Scripture, praying persistently, and placing our faith in the perfect will of God.

A PERSONAL TESTIMONY OF UNSHAKABLE FAITH: TRUSTING GOD AMID DOUBT AND FEAR

The story behind this book is nothing short of a miracle. For over two years, I had this feeling that God was pushing me gently to take up the task of writing a book. Yet, time and again, self-doubt kept me frozen, and the idea remained just that—an idea. And it's in those exact moments that God reminds me, through His Word, of a very pivotal thing: *"For God has not given us a spirit of fear, but of power and of love and of a sound mind."* **2 Timothy 1:7 NKJV.** A truth that served to chip down my fear-that truth and the fact courage is from Him, not just merely or entirely from personal strength.

It was in those quiet moments of prayer and reflection that I began to feel this still, small voice within me. Not loud, not demanding, yet persistent and insistent-this was something I was to do. And, of course, that makes me think of the story of Elijah: *"And after the earthquake a fire, but the Lord was not in the fire; and after the fire a still small voice."* **1 King 19:12 NKJV.** It was in that gentle nudge I recognized God's unmistakable call.

Even at that, knowing full well, I contended with mine. I turned to the Holy Spirit to make sense with questions in my heart. One prayer became my refrain: **"Lord, if it is really Your will for me to write a book, please show me the title."** I clung to the promise in **Jeremiah 33.3 NKJV**: *"Call to Me, and I will answer you, and show you great and mighty things, which you do not know."* Though the answer didn't come right away, I held onto the truth of **Ecclesiastes 3:11 NKJV**, *"He has made everything beautiful in its time. Also, He has put eternity in their hearts, except that no one can find out the work that God does from beginning to end."*

Then one morning was different. Sharply at 4:18 a.m., I woke up to a still, small, undeniable whisper in my heart: **"The Power of Unshakable Faith."** The words pierced deep, and I knew right then and there this was it- the divine answer I had been seeking. **Isaiah 30:21 NKJV** sprang to mind: *"Your ears shall hear a word behind you, saying, 'This is the way, walk in it,' whenever you turn to the right hand or whenever you turn to the left."* Smitten with gratefulness and wonder, I did not let one fragment of this holy moment get away as I hastened for my phone to jot down the title.

Empowered with a new sense of purpose, I sat at my computer and began to write. The words came-the act of surrender, as if God Himself was guiding each thought. **Proverbs 3:5-6 NKJV** became my anchor: *"Trust in the Lord* *with all your heart and lean not on your own understanding; in all your ways acknowledge Him, and He shall direct your paths."*

This book is more than a project; it is a calling fulfilled, a testimony to God's guidance, and a living reflection of what it is to walk in faith despite lingering doubts. Each step of this journey has reminded me of **Ephesians 3:20 NKJV,** *"Now to Him who is able to do exceedingly abundantly above all that we ask or think, according to the power that works in us."* Indeed, it has been a journey undergirded by His power, faithfulness, and unending grace.

Conclusion

Doubt and fear are common human emotions that typically surface when we stand on the brink of the unknown or face life's most difficult challenges. These emotions, while unavoidable, do not have to define or control our lives. In moments of uncertainty, we are encouraged to confront our concerns with courage, seek solace in earnest prayer, and take strength from Jesus Christ's example. His unwavering faith in God's divine plan acts as both a guiding beacon and a tremendous source of inspiration, reminding us that faith triumphs over fear.

Through prayer and surrender, we find the strength to push past fear and uncertainty, standing firm on the promises of God. Jesus is the ultimate example of trust and faith, especially in times of distress and challenge. From His trials in the wilderness to His agonizing prayer in Gethsemane, Jesus showed us that faith is not the absence of fear or doubt, but the courage to trust in God's will regardless of the circumstances. Even in the face of the ultimate sacrifice, He never wavered in His belief that God's plan was good and just, teaching us that through faith, we too can emerge victorious over life's most daunting obstacles.

As we continue our journey of faith, let us remember that God's promises are steadfast and unchanging. His presence is ever with us, guiding and supporting us through every storm. His power is greater than any fear or doubt we may encounter, and through His strength, we can rise above every challenge. By keeping our focus on His truth and leaning into His promises, we are equipped to navigate life's uncertainties with unshakable faith. Through Him, we are more than conquerors, and through faith, we can overcome all things.

A PRAYER: OVERCOMING DOUBT AND FEAR WITH FAITH

Heavenly Father,

I come before You today, humbly acknowledging Your supreme authority over all things. I place my trust in Your boundless power to overcome the doubts and fears that seek to hinder me. You are the One who calms the storms, strengthens the weary, and delivers the anxious and afraid. In You, I find refuge and strength, and in Your presence, fear cannot abide.

Lord, I stand on the truth of **2 Timothy 1:7 NKJV,** which declares, *"For God has not given us a spirit of fear, but of power and of love and of a sound* *mind."* I thank You, Lord, for the spirit of strength and courage You have imparted to me, dispelling fear with Your divine empowerment. I choose to reject the lies of fear and doubt that seek to take root in my heart, embracing instead the boldness and resilience that Your Holy Spirit provides.

I hold firmly to the promise of **Isaiah 41:10 NKJV,** which reassures us, *"Fear not, for I am with you; Be not dismayed, for I am your God. I will strengthen you, yes, I will help you, I will uphold you with my righteous right hand."* Father, when fear rises within me, remind me that You are with me, strengthening and sustaining me with Your mighty hand. With You by my side, there is nothing to fear.

I recall the words of Jesus in **Matthew 17:20 NKJV,** where He says, *"If you have faith as a mustard seed, you will say to this mountain, 'Move from here to there,' and it will move; and nothing will be impossible for you."* Even in the face of doubt, help me remember that even the smallest seed of faith can move mountains. Lord, increase my faith and teach me to trust You in every circumstance.

When fear threatens to overwhelm my heart, I declare the truth of **Psalm 56:3 NKJV,** *"Whenever I am afraid, I will trust in You."* I will not allow fear to govern me, for I place my complete trust in You, the One who is unwavering and faithful. You are my security and my peace.

Father, I rest in Your promise from **Philippians 4:6-7 NKJV,** *"Be anxious for nothing, but in everything by prayer and supplication, with* *thanksgiving, let your requests be made known to God; and the peace of God, which surpasses understanding, will guard your hearts and minds through Christ Jesus."* When anxiety seeks to rob me of peace, I will bring my concerns to You in prayer, trusting You to guard my heart and mind with Your perfect peace.

I claim the words of Jesus from **John 14:27 NKJV**: *"Peace I leave with you; my peace I give you; not as the world gives do I give to you. Let not your heart be troubled, neither let it be afraid."* Lord, I receive the peace of Christ, a peace that surpasses all understanding. I will not allow my heart to be troubled, for Your peace reigns within me.

Thank You, Lord, for the power of Your presence, which drives out all fear. As Your Word assures us in **1 John 4:18 NKJV,** *"There is no fear in love; but perfect love cast out fear, because fear involves torment. But he who fears has not been made perfect in love."* I thank You that Your perfect love casts out all fear. I open my heart to receive Your love today, allowing it to replace every doubt and worry with unshakable confidence in Your perfect plan for my life.

Lord, I choose to walk by faith, not by sight**.** I trust that You are working in my life, even when I cannot see the full picture. I refuse to be governed by fear or doubt, and I stand firm on the promises You have made. I know that You are faithful to complete the work You have begun in me.

Thank You, Father, for Your love, peace, and strength. I declare that through Christ, I am more than a conqueror, and I will overcome all fear and doubt through the power of Your Word and the strength of Your Spirit.

In the mighty name of Jesus, the One who has overcome the world, I pray.

Amen.

CHAPTER FIVE
FAITH THAT MOVES MOUNTAINS

Faith is certainly one of humanity's most extraordinary and transforming forces—a powerful yet invisible force capable of reshaping lives, turning bad situations around, and breaking down seemingly insurmountable obstacles.

Its power comes not from simple human determination, but from a divine link to God, the source of all miracles and the one who makes the unthinkable a reality. Scripture is replete with amazing anecdotes about people whose lives were dramatically impacted by their unshakeable faith.

These examples demonstrate that faith not only inspires hope, but also activates the miraculous. These stories demonstrate the limitless power of trusting in God, from healing the ill and repairing broken lives to reviving the dead.

The Bible is full of exciting stories about amazing events that occurred because of faith, but the concept of "mountain-moving faith" challenges us to dig further. What does it really mean to have faith that can move mountains? Is it simply believing in the impossible, or does it speak to a deeper and more transforming understanding of faith—one that must be accepted in order to truly experience its power?

To understand the essence of this exceptional faith, we must first recognize that it cannot be learned in an instant. True faith necessitates ongoing effort, deliberate practice, and unwavering dedication to God. It is not a transitory emotion but rather a virtue developed over time via prayer, Bible study, and a heart attuned to God's desire. This process of fostering faith is essential for spiritual growth, strengthening our link with God and revealing the depths of His character.

The teachings of Scripture, combined with the testimony of those who came before us, demonstrate that mountain-moving faith goes beyond the act of asking for miracles. It is founded on trusting God's timetable, relying on His wisdom, and placing complete faith in His ability to intercede on our behalf. Such faith affects our perspective, teaching us that true strength is found not only in the outcomes we desire but also in our trust in the One who holds the mountains in His hands.

The Scriptures provide extensive information about the nature of religion. Jesus frequently stressed the power of faith, especially in confrontations with those seeking healing and release. In **Matthew 17:20 NKJV,** Jesus tells His disciples, *"If you have faith as a mustard seed, you will say to this mountain, 'Move from here to there,' and it will move; and nothing will be impossible for you."*

This passage is not necessarily about the literal moving of physical mountains but rather about the kind of unshakable faith that can overcome any challenge or obstacle that stands in our way. Jesus' statements underline that the size of the faith is not as significant as the object of that faith—God Himself. When our confidence is anchored in God, even the smallest bit of faith can generate spectacular outcomes.

Faith that moves mountains is built in an unbreakable trust that continues throughout life's challenges and disappointments. It is the kind of faith that dares to believe in God's promises, even when the route ahead seems obscure, or the outcome appears impossible.

This faith fosters confidence, motivating us to move forward in the direction God directs, no matter how difficult the journey may appear. It does not retreat in the face of adversity but presses on, rooted in the conviction that God is far larger than any scenario we confront. Whether we are navigating personal hardships, mending broken relationships, overcoming financial obstacles, or dealing with health issues, mountain-moving faith allows us to persist, knowing that God is working behind the scenes, even while the larger picture is concealed.

Mountain-moving faith is fundamentally tied to the transformational power of prayer. Through constant and passionate prayer, we move closer to God's heart, seeking His will and aligning our goals with His divine plans.

Prayer becomes more than a ritual or a list of requests; it is a sacred dialogue through which we express our confidence, surrender, and reliance on His wisdom and grace. When we pray with faith, we admit our human limits and put our trust in God's limitless ability to intervene in ways beyond our comprehension.

Faith and prayer work together to produce a powerful synergy, preparing us to meet life's problems with fortitude and hope. As we lean into these heavenly gifts, we are reminded that even the tiniest act of faith, when offered with sincerity, can result in astonishing outcomes when placed in the hands of an all-mighty God.

The influence of mountain-moving faith goes well beyond personal transformation. When we walk by faith, we not only experience God's power in our own lives, but we also become channels through which His power might flow to others. Our faith can inspire and encourage people around us, leading them to God as a source of hope and promise. Real-life testimonies demonstrate how faith's remarkable power can alter entire communities, mend fractured relationships, and restore broken lives.

In this chapter, we will look at the essence of "mountain-moving faith"—a faith that is so steadfast and powerful that it can overcome any challenge, no matter how intimidating, big, or seemingly impenetrable. This type of faith is not a transitory or superficial conviction but rather a deep, persistent trust in God that enables people to act in the face of hardship and challenge. It is the type of faith that, when completely matured and nurtured, allows people to look beyond their immediate circumstances and trust in God's larger plan and purpose for them.

Mountain-moving faith is more than simply believing that things will improve; it is about aligning our hearts and minds with God's will and trusting that His power is greater than any obstacle we may encounter.

THE POWER OF FAITH: MORE THAN JUST BELIEVING

In the Gospel of **Matthew 17:20 NKJV**, Jesus makes a statement to His disciples that may appear almost unbelievable at first glance: *"If you have faith as a mustard seed, you will say to this mountain, 'Move from here to there,' and it will move; and nothing will be impossible for you."* On the surface, this may appear exaggerated, or even unrealistic; after all, how can anyone move a physical mountain with nothing but faith?

However, within this statement lies a profound and powerful spiritual truth—one that transcends the literal interpretation and reveals a deeper, more transformative understanding of faith. What Jesus is conveying is not a promise that we will literally be able to relocate mountains with a few words, but rather that faith has the extraordinary potential to overcome the seemingly insurmountable obstacles and trials that we face in our lives. The "mountains" in our lives represent challenges—be they personal, relational, financial, or spiritual—that appear to be too great for us to handle. Jesus is illustrating the profound power of faith in God to help us overcome these challenges.

At the core of this teaching is the understanding that faith is not measured by its size, but by its object. In other words, it is not the quantity of our faith that matters, but the quality of what—and more importantly, *who*—we place our faith in. Jesus emphasizes that even a small amount of faith, as small as a mustard seed, when placed in the hands of an omnipotent God, has the potential to move mountains.

The lesson here is not about the size or strength of our faith but about the greatness and power of the One in whom we place our trust. Faith is not about the individual's capacity to believe, but about the power of God to act through that belief. This is a fundamental distinction that separates mere belief from the transformative power of true, biblical faith.

Jesus' description of faith is not one of passive believing or wishful thinking, in which one expects the best. It is an active confidence, a profound dependence on God's authority and strength. Faith in God entails placing our complete trust in His power to intervene and act in ways that we cannot fully explain or predict.

It is the assurance that, no matter how intractable our issues appear to be, God is capable of working through and with us to overcome them. This type of faith is based on God's limitless and unwavering power rather than our abilities or strengths. The Bible makes it clear in numerous passages that faith is a means by which we tap into God's power and allow that power to work in and through our lives.

Furthermore, Jesus' comments in **Matthew 17:20 NKJV** should prompt us to consider what it truly means to have faith in God. In modern society, religion is frequently reduced to mere belief—an intellectual agreement with specific concepts or systems. However, biblical faith goes much deeper than this.

It is more than just a mental ascension to a set of truths; it is a genuine belief in a live and active God. Faith entails submitting our understanding and goals to God's perfect will. It takes a willing heart to trust God, even when the route ahead is unclear, or the circumstances appear overwhelming. This kind of faith does not shy away from obstacles but boldly confronts them, trusting that God will provide a way through.

One of the most difficult problems in developing this type of faith is the propensity to put our reliance on our own skills or on the fleeting things of this world. When everything appears to be going well, we rely on our power, resources, and understanding.

True faith, on the other hand, is frequently tested and refined throughout times of adversity, uncertainty, and doubt. During these times, we are encouraged to lean into God's power, recognizing that He is greater than any difficulty we encounter.

This is when faith's transformational power shines through. It allows us to rise above our circumstances, not because we are strong or capable in our own right, but because we know that God's strength is made perfect in our weakness.

Faith that moves mountains is not about achieving personal greatness or receiving everything we ask for. It is about aligning our hearts with God's will and trusting that His plans for us are good, even when we cannot see the result.

It is the willingness to believe that God will provide for us, guide us, and equip us to face whatever challenges arise, no matter how impossible they may seem. This is the faith that enables believers to step out in obedience, even when the road ahead is uncertain or when the task before them appears overwhelming. It is the kind of faith that enabled Abraham to leave his homeland without knowing where he was going and the kind of faith that empowered David to face the giant Goliath with nothing but a sling and a stone.

To cultivate this mountain-moving faith, we must intentionally focus on deepening our relationship with God. Faith is not something that can be generated through human effort alone. Rather, it grows and flourishes when we seek God earnestly through prayer, Scripture, and worship. It is nourished when we reflect on His past faithfulness and recognize the many ways He has worked in our lives.

As our trust in God deepens, we begin to see the impossible become possible. We begin to realize that God's power is not confined by our limitations, but that He can use even our smallest steps of faith to bring about great things.

Moreover, the power of faith goes beyond individual experiences and extends into the lives of those around us. Just as Jesus demonstrated the impact of faith through His own ministry, believers are called to live out their faith in ways that inspire and encourage others.

When we demonstrate faith in action—by trusting God in difficult circumstances, by believing in His promises despite the challenges we face—we become a testimony to others of His goodness, faithfulness, and power. Our faith can move not only mountains in our own lives but also influence the lives of others, drawing them closer to God and encouraging them to believe that, with God, all things are possible.

The power of faith that Jesus speaks of is not merely a belief in abstract concepts, but a dynamic, life-transforming trust in God's ability to work in our lives and through us. Faith that moves mountains is not about the size or strength of our belief, but about the object of that belief—God Himself.

It is the faith that enables us to confront the challenges of life with confidence, knowing that God is with us and that His power can overcome any obstacle. As we cultivate this kind of faith, we open ourselves to the extraordinary possibilities that God has in store for us. In every circumstance, no matter how overwhelming, we can trust that with God, nothing is impossible.

UNDERSTANDING MOUNTAIN-MOVING FAITH

Mountain-moving faith is not passive or weak. It is a bold, active faith that engages fully with the promises of God. It refuses to bow to fear or doubt and stands firm even in the face of opposition. In **Mark 11:23 NKJV,** Jesus emphasizes the importance of unwavering belief: *"Have faith in God. For assuredly I say to you, whoever says to this mountain, "Be removed and be cast into the sea,' and does not doubt in his heart, but believes that those things he says will be done, he will have whatever he says."* This powerful verse underscores the necessity of belief without doubt, trusting wholeheartedly in God's ability to overcome the obstacles before us.

To cultivate this kind of faith, we must understand that it requires more than just wishful thinking or empty hopes. Mountain-moving faith is built on certain foundational elements:

Trusting in God's Promises

Faith that moves mountains is anchored in a deep and unshakable trust in God's Word. We must believe that His promises are sure and that He is faithful to fulfill them, no matter the circumstances. Our faith is built not on fleeting emotions, but on the eternal reliability of God.

Standing Firm in Prayer

True mountain-moving faith requires persistent and confident prayer. As Jesus teaches in **Mark 11:24 NJKV,** when we pray, we must ask in faith, believing that God will answer according to His will and timing. Prayer is the avenue through which we connect with God, aligning our hearts with His divine plan.

Taking Action

Faith is not passive—it is active. As **James 2:26 NKJV** reminds us, *"For as the body without the spirit is dead, so faith without works is dead also."* Genuine faith compels us to act in alignment with our beliefs. Even when the path ahead seems unclear, mountain-moving faith moves us to step forward, trusting that God will direct our steps and guide us through every challenge.

Mountain-moving faith is not about relying on our own strength, nor is it an exercise in self-deception. It is about aligning our hearts with God's will, trusting that His power is greater than any challenge we may face, and stepping forward in obedience, knowing that He will move the mountains in our lives.

THE IMPORTANCE OF PERSEVERANCE IN FAITH

One of the most important characteristics of mountain-moving faith is perseverance. Faith, in its genuine biblical definition, is more than just a single moment of believing or a transitory emotion; it is a constant, enduring process of relying in God, especially when the outcome is not immediately apparent, or the route appears uncertain.

The Bible continually promotes the idea that faith is dynamic and ever-changing, rather than passive or stagnant. Perseverance, in times of both triumph and trial, makes our faith firm and unwavering.

The ability of faith to move mountains is not a question of initial belief but one of persistence in endurance through challenges and hardships. In **Luke 17:5-6 NKJV,** the apostles asked Jesus to increase their faith, and He answered them by reminding them that even a small amount of faith, as small as a mustard seed, can achieve the impossible.

This verse teaches us a valuable lesson concerning the nature of faith-it is not how much conviction one has, but it is a matter of constancy and quality over time.

Even the smallest seed of trust, when cultivated and persevered in, can yield huge results. Faith, then, is not only about obtaining benefits or seeing immediate responses to prayer; it is about having a deeper relationship with God that is built in trust, submission, and unshakeable belief that He is working, even when we cannot yet see His work unfolding before us.

In **Romans 5:3-4 NKJV**, the Apostle Paul gives us one of those expanded understandings in the life of a believer: *"And not only that, but we also glory in tribulations, knowing that tribulation produces perseverance; and perseverance, character; and character, hope."* This chapter provides an essential, truthful reality about suffering and hardship in the Christian life.

It is through hardships that God polishes our faith and character, not punishes us. Sufferings, whether personal, relational, or external, are more than just barriers to overcome; they are chances for God to mold us, draw us closer to Him, and build the very faith that will sustain us in future tribulations.

Suffering provides us with a significant opportunity to persevere—to maintain our faith in God even when the way ahead appears uncertain or daunting. Perseverance becomes a refining process, molding our personalities and fostering virtues such as patience, endurance, humility, and resilience. These characteristics not only strengthen us, but also prepare us to face future trials with a renewed feeling of optimism and steadfast faith in God's goodness.

Faith persistence entails much more than simply enduring adversity with stoic quiet or hesitant acceptance. It is an active, conscious faith in God's goodness, His unchanging promises, and His ability to carry out His intentions, even when the circumstances around us appear to contradict our beliefs.

It is through this active perseverance that our faith becomes stronger and more resilient. As we continue to trust God despite difficulties, our hearts are transformed, and our character is refined. The trials we face no longer become sources of despair, but stepping stones in our journey toward greater spiritual maturity and deeper intimacy with God.

The relationship between perseverance and character development is crucial in understanding the power of enduring faith. Just as a tree's roots grow deeper and stronger during storms, so too does our faith grow deeper and more established during times of adversity. The process of perseverance cultivates in us the ability to stand firm, rooted in the knowledge that God is with us, even in the most challenging of times.

This deeper faith is not one that is shaken by every wind of change or every hardship but one that remains firm and confident, trusting that God will ultimately work all things together for our good. As we persevere, we are shaped more and more into the image of Christ, developing character traits that reflect His love, compassion, and strength.

The process of perseverance in faith also develops hope—the kind of hope that does not disappoint or falter in the face of trials. **Romans 5:4 NKJV** concludes with the powerful statement that *"and perseverance, character; and character, hope."* Hope is not merely wishful thinking or a vague sense of optimism; it is a confident expectation based on God's promises and faithfulness. As our faith grows through perseverance, we develop a hope that is anchored not in our circumstances but in the unchanging nature of God.

This hope enables us to face future challenges with unwavering confidence, knowing that God will see us through, just as He has been faithful in the past. Hope, therefore, is the fruit of perseverance, and it is through this hope that we find the strength to endure and to trust God in all things.

Faith that perseveres is a faith that matures and deepens over time. The greater the trial, the greater the opportunity for growth. In the same way that physical muscles grow stronger through resistance and exertion, our spiritual muscles grow through the trials and hardships we face.

Each challenge, each moment of hardship, is an opportunity to trust God more deeply, to rely on His strength rather than our own, and to experience His presence in ways that we could not in times of ease. It is through these moments of perseverance that we develop the qualities that enable us to move forward with greater confidence in God's ability to move mountains in our lives.

Moreover, perseverance in faith is not just a personal journey; it has profound implications for the broader Christian community. When we persevere in our faith, we become witnesses to others of God's faithfulness and power.

Our endurance amid trials can serve as an encouragement to others who are facing their own struggles, providing them with the strength to press on and trust in God's provision. The body of Christ is called to bear one another's burdens and to encourage one another in the faith. Through our perseverance, we can become instruments of encouragement, lifting up those who may be struggling in their own journeys of faith.

Perseverance is a vital component of mountain-moving faith. It is through perseverance that our faith grows stronger, our character is refined, and our hope is anchored in God's promises. Just as a tree's roots grow deeper in the storm, so too does our faith grow stronger in times of trial. The process of perseverance is not easy, but it is through these challenges that our trust in God deepens, and we become more like Christ.

As we endure and persevere, we develop the resilience and strength needed to face future challenges with confidence, knowing that God is always with us, working all things together for our good. Perseverance in faith is not simply about enduring hardship; it is about actively trusting God and allowing Him to shape us into the image of Christ, so that we may move mountains and live out our calling with unwavering faith.

BIBLICAL STORIES OF MOUNTAIN-MOVING FAITH

Where faith has been deeply rooted in God, the dissolution of barriers, the healing of the broken, and the way for astonishing miracles are paved. Such is faith that we repeatedly see, throughout Scripture, the stories of those whose mountain-moving faith in God's promises enables them to see the impossible. These accounts of mountain-moving faith remain a timeless call to wholeheartedly trust God, no matter the seemingly insurmountable obstacles.

Let us look at some of the most astounding Bible stories in which faith not only inspired but also illustrated how God's power affects lives in ways that are beyond human comprehension. Each story highlights the transformative power of unwavering faith, challenging us to consider the limitless possibilities that arise when we put our trust in Him. These are not mere recorded history, but living examples to show how God acts in the life of a person who trusts in Him, turning adversities into victories and impossibilities into possibilities.

The Healing of the Paralytic: Faith That Breaks Barriers (Mark 2:1-12 NKJV)

One of the most compelling demonstrations of faith in action is found in the story of the paralyzed man whose friends took extraordinary steps to bring him before Jesus. Unable to reach Jesus on his own due to his paralysis, the man's friends exhibited remarkable faith, going so far as to lower him through a roof to ensure he had an opportunity for healing. Jesus, witnessing their bold faith, responded by healing the man, saying, *"Son, your sins are forgiven... I say to you, arise, take up your bed, and go to your house."*

This account teaches us several lessons. First, the faith of the paralytic's friends moved Jesus to act in a miraculous way. Their belief in Jesus' healing power led them to take risks and break through physical and social barriers. It wasn't just the man's faith that mattered, but the collective faith of his friends, which became the catalyst for his healing. This story encourages us to not only believe in God's power but to actively pursue solutions, even when the obstacles seem insurmountable.

The Faith of the Centurion: Believing Beyond Boundaries (Matthew 8:5-13 NKJV)

In another profound example of faith, a Roman centurion came to Jesus, seeking healing for his servant. Rather than asking Jesus to come to his house, the centurion expressed an extraordinary belief in Jesus' ability to heal from a distance. *"Lord I am not worthy that You should come under my roof. But only speak the word, and my servant will be healed,"* he said. Jesus, amazed by his faith, healed the servant without physically being present.

This story reveals that faith is not confined by location or physical proximity to Jesus. It transcends circumstances, highlighting that the power of God is not limited by space or time. The centurion understood the authority of Jesus and trusted that a single word from Him could bring healing. This testimony encourages us to place our faith not in what we can see or understand, but in the omnipotent power of God that works beyond our human limitations.

The Resurrection of Lazarus: Faith that Conquers Death (John 11:1-44 NKJV)

The resurrection of Lazarus is perhaps one of the most dramatic examples of mountain-moving faith in the Bible. Lazarus had been dead for four days, and his sisters, Mary and Martha, were mourning his loss. They had faith that Jesus could have healed him if He had arrived sooner, but they struggled to believe that Jesus could raise him from the dead. However, Jesus, moved by compassion and demonstrating His power over death, called Lazarus out of the tomb, restoring him to life.

Before performing this miracle, Jesus asked Martha, *"Did I not say to you that if you would believe you would see the glory of God?"* This statement underscores the connection between faith and God's miraculous power. The resurrection of Lazarus was not just a demonstration of Jesus' authority over life and death but also a testimony to the transformative nature of faith. This story teaches us that faith can bring about radical change, even in situations where all seems lost. When we trust God, even in the face of death or despair, we open ourselves to witnessing His glory in ways that defy logic and expectations.

The Woman with the Issue of Blood: Faith that Seizes Opportunity (Mark 5:25-34 NKJV)

Another powerful story of faith is that of the woman who had been suffering from a bleeding condition for twelve years. Having spent all her money on doctors with no improvement, she believed that if she could just touch the hem of Jesus' garment, she would be healed. Her faith was active—she didn't wait for Jesus to come to her; instead, she took decisive action and sought Him out in a crowd, believing that His power could heal her.

When she touched His garment, Jesus immediately felt power leave Him, and the woman was healed. He turned to her and said, *"Daughter, your faith has made you well. Go in peace and be healed of your affliction."* This moment reveals the profound connection between faith and action. The woman's belief was not a passive hope; it was an active trust in Jesus' ability to heal. Her faith not only healed her physically but also restored her spiritually and emotionally, transforming her life. Her story serves as a reminder that faith often requires us to take bold steps, even when the path ahead is unclear.

The Healing of Blind Bartimaeus (Mark 10:46-52 NKJV)

One of the most profound demonstrations of mountain-moving faith is found in the story of Bartimaeus, a blind man who sat by the roadside near Jericho. When he heard that Jesus was passing by, he cried out, *"Jesus, Son of David, have mercy on me!"* Despite being told by the crowd to remain silent, Bartimaeus' faith remained unwavering. He did not let the voices of others silence his plea for healing. He believed deeply that Jesus had the power to heal him, even in the face of his blindness.

Jesus, moved by his persistence, stopped and called for him to be brought forward. When Bartimaeus stood before Jesus, He asked, *"What do you want me to do for you?"* Bartimaeus boldly requested, *"Rabboni, that I may receive my sight."* In response, Jesus told him, *"Go your way; your faith has made you well."* Immediately, Bartimaeus' sight was restored, and he followed Jesus, praising God.

This powerful story shows us that mountain-moving faith is not deterred by the doubts or distractions around us. Bartimaeus' unshakeable belief in

Jesus' ability to heal him—despite his circumstances—was the key to his miracle. His faith was not passive; it was active, persistent, and unwavering. Through his trust in the power of Jesus, he experienced a life-changing miracle.

The Faith of Abraham (Genesis 22:1-19 NKJV)

Perhaps one of the most extraordinary stories of mountain-moving faith is the account of Abraham's willingness to sacrifice his son, Isaac, in obedience to God's command. In Genesis 22, God tests Abraham's faith by instructing him to take Isaac, the promised child, to the mountain and offer him as a sacrifice. This command must have been a deep challenge to Abraham, for Isaac was the son through whom God had promised to make him the father of many nations.

Yet, Abraham's faith in God's promises was so steadfast that he obeyed without hesitation. He trusted that God, who had promised to fulfill His covenant through Isaac, would somehow provide a way. As Abraham prepared to sacrifice Isaac on the altar, God intervened and provided a ram as a substitute offering. Abraham's obedience and faith in God's provision demonstrated an unwavering trust in God's plan, even when the outcome seemed unclear.

This powerful story reveals that mountain-moving faith is rooted in complete trust in God's will, even when the path ahead is shrouded in uncertainty. Abraham's faith wasn't based on his understanding of the situation, but on his complete confidence in God's character and promises.

His willingness to obey God, even in the most difficult of circumstances, became a pivotal moment in his faith journey, and it is a testimony to us all.

These biblical accounts demonstrate that faith that moves mountains is not about passive hope, but active, persistent trust in God's power and promises. Whether it is through the unwavering persistence of Bartimaeus, the bold action of the woman with the issue of blood, or the complete surrender of Abraham, we learn that mountain-moving faith requires courage, action, and an unshakeable belief in God's ability to do the impossible. In our own lives, when faced with obstacles that seem insurmountable, we are called to embody the same kind of faith—believing that with God, all things are possible.

SHIFTING FOCUS: FROM MOUNTAINS TO THE MOUNTAIN-MOVER

A significant lesson from Jesus' teachings reminds us that the scale of our challenges—the mountains we face—is not what is most important. Our God's magnificence is what gives us power. Far too often, we allow ourselves to be overwhelmed by the enormity of our issues, focused entirely on the challenges ahead of us.

Yet, when we lift our eyes from the mountain and fix them on the Almighty God we serve, everything changes. This is the Creator of the universe—the One who breathed life into existence—and He assures us that He stands with us in every trial.

As we face the challenges in life, faith urges us to focus not on the size of the obstacle but on the boundless power of God. When we place our faith in His omnipotence, we begin to see that what once seemed like an insurmountable barrier is, in reality, an opportunity for God to display His greatness.

The story of **David and Goliath** is a perfect example of this principle. David, a youthful shepherd, defeated the giant Goliath not by focusing on his size, but by believing in the might of the God he served **1 Samuel 17 NKJV**. Like David, we are called to face our trials with the assurance that our God is larger than any giant we might encounter.

THE TRANSFORMATIVE NATURE OF FAITH

Faith is much more than a belief system; it is a dynamic, transformational force that changes the way we think, feel, and live. When we put our belief in God's ability to move mountains, it doesn't just change our circumstances; it transforms us from within. Faith has the astonishing potential to transform our perspectives, replacing fear with courage, uncertainty with unshakeable confidence, and despair with renewed hope. While faith does not deny the reality of life's difficulties, it does enable us to overcome them, reminding us that God's greatness outweighs any difficulty we may face.

Faith is peace, even when a storm is raging around you, the most terrible of life's storms. For as **Philippians 4:6-7 NKJV** reminds, we are to lay our burdens at the feet of God, who will replace them with a peace that surpasses comprehension. This unshakable faith reminds us of the sovereignty of God in the affairs of life and His ever-present nature.

It empowers us to confront challenges with steadfast courage, confident that He will not only provide for our needs but also guide us through every trial with His unfailing love and wisdom.

A PERSONAL TESTIMONY OF FAITH THAT MOVES MOUNTAINS: NOT GIVING UP ON MY AMERICAN DREAM

A delicate yet bright dream has burned softly within me since I was a child. I yearned for the **"American Dream,"** not only for myself, but also for the optimism it represented for my family. This was not a passing fancy; it was a profound desire that I conveyed to God in hushed prayers as a child, loud cries as a teenager, and weeping pleadings as a young adult kneeling in church. I held to **Psalms 37:4 NKJV** promise: *"Delight yourself in the Lord, and He shall give you the desires of your heart."*

At 21, it seemed that the doors to my dream were finally opening. I was accepted into a program that offered a pathway to the United States, passing the interview process with a heart full of hope. My grandparents, who had raised me with boundless love and sacrifices, offered to sell a treasured piece of farmland to cover the financial requirements. Their selflessness brought tears to my eyes, a tangible expression of their unwavering belief in me.

But joy quickly turned to turmoil. My uncles and aunts, fueled by anger and misunderstanding, fiercely opposed the plan. Their harsh words echoed in my heart, *"Why would you sell the farm for her? She's just your grandchild!"* Each word was a knife to my spirit, casting shadows of doubt over my worth and my dreams. Yet even in this, I chose to forgive, holding onto **Colossians 3:13 NKJV**: *"bearing with one another, and forgiving one another, if anyone has a complaint against another; even as Christ forgave you, so you also must do."*

The love of my grandparents stood unshaken, but I could not bear to see their hearts burdened by conflict. With trembling hands and an aching soul, I made the most painful decision of my life. I stepped away from the program, surrendering the dream I had nurtured for so long. It felt like a part of me had been torn away, yet I held firmly to the promise of **Romans 8:28 NKJV***: "And we know that all things work together for good to those who love God, to those who are the called according to His purpose."*

The years that followed were a quiet season of waiting and trusting. By the age of 28, I had poured myself into teaching—a calling that brought purpose but left the dream of America quietly tucked away. Then, out of nowhere, came a text message from an unknown number. It spoke of U.S. employers coming to Manila to interview teachers. Doubt crept in immediately. *"It's probably a scam,"* I thought. But deep within me, a small voice urged, *what if this is God's plan?*

With a spark of faith, I traveled to Manila and attended the job fair. The moment I sat in the interview chair, I felt an overwhelming peace, as if God Himself was guiding every word I spoke. When I passed the interview, my heart swelled with joy, but challenges still loomed large. Financial resources seemed out of reach, but God, as always, proved faithful. Through unexpected blessings, loans, and divine provision, every obstacle was overcome.

Finally, in September 2008, I stood on American soil for the first time. Tears streamed down my face as I realized the fullness of God's faithfulness. What began as a prayer, carried through years of heartache and sacrifice, had become a reality. The words of **Ephesians 3:20 NKJV** came alive in my heart: *"Now to Him who is able to do exceedingly abundantly above all that we ask or think, according to the power that works in us."*

Looking back, I view each tear, trial, and waiting moment as a thread in the beautiful tapestry of God's design for my life. **Hebrews 11:1 NKJV** became my rock: *"Now faith is the substance of things hoped for, the evidence of things not seen."* My journey was never about me; it was always about God's glory and His unchanging promises.

To anyone reading this, let my story remind you of this truth: God's timing is perfect, His plans are good, and His love never fails. Trust Him, even when the road seems impossible. He is the God who turns mourning into dancing, dreams into reality, and faith into miracles. Hold onto Him, for He will never let you go. In His perfect time, He will make a way.

Conclusion

Faith that moves mountains is about actively putting our trust in God's power, even in the face of terrible circumstances. It is not just about believing the impossible. It is about understanding that, despite our inability to perceive the outcomes, God is constantly at work.

I learned from my experience that mountain-moving faith is more than just a wish; it is a firm belief in God's sovereignty, based on the conviction that He is always working for our good, no matter what. We access a power beyond human comprehension when we put our faith in Jesus Christ. God works in our lives via our faith, bringing about breakthroughs, healing, provision, and restoration. God's strength is bigger than any challenge or mountain we may face, whether it is illness, loss, or uncertainty. His promises are fulfilled, and His love and fidelity are unwavering.

As we walk in trust, we are reminded that no task is too big for God. God can use His strength and grace to get us through any difficult situation, whether it's a great valley of grief or an apparently impassable mountain. Even when the future is uncertain, He asks us to have faith in Him. We can encounter His supernatural power in ways that will transform our lives forever if we hold fast to His promises, pray fervently, and maintain our faith.

When faith is in the hands of the Almighty, it may change situations, cure the sick, and mend relationships. One prayer at a time can transform the world. Knowing that all is possible with God, let's live out that faith every day. His power is limitless, and His love endures even in the face of suffering and loss.

A PRAYER: FAITH THAT MOVES MOUNTAINS

Heavenly Father,

I come before You with a heart full of faith, trusting in Your boundless power to move mountains. I know, Lord, that with You, all things are possible, and I believe that nothing can stand in the way of Your will. I place my trust in Your Word, for You have blessed me with the gift of faith to overcome every obstacle I face.

I hold fast to the truth of **Matthew 17:20 NKJV**, where Jesus reminds us that even faith as small as a mustard seed has the power to move mountains. I am grateful, Lord, that with just a little faith, I can see Your miraculous work in my life. I ask today that You increase my faith, helping me to trust You completely, regardless of the size of the challenges before me.

Father, I declare the promise found in **Mark 11:23 NKJV**, where Jesus tells us that if we speak to a mountain with unwavering belief, it will be cast into the sea. I stand firm in this promise, knowing that by faith, every obstacle in my life is subject to Your will. I refuse to doubt but instead choose to trust in Your Word, knowing that Your promises are always true.

Thank You, Lord, for the assurance of **Luke 1:37 NKJV,** which declares, *"For with God nothing will be impossible.",* I stand on this truth, confident that Your Word holds the power to transform every circumstance I face. When challenges arise, I will remain grounded in Your promises, knowing that You are faithful, and Your Word never returns void.

As I pray today, I remember the words of **Matthew 21:22 NKJV,** where Jesus assures us*," And whatever things you ask in prayer, believing, you will receive."* I come before You with unwavering faith, believing that You hear my prayers and will answer them in alignment with Your perfect will. I trust in **Ephesians 3:20 NKJV**, which reminds us that You are able to do exceedingly abundantly above all that we ask or think, according to the power that works in us.

Lord, I surrender my doubts and fears to You, for I know they have no place in a heart that is filled with faith. Even when I cannot see the way ahead, I trust that You are working on my behalf. As **Hebrews 11:1 NKJV** tells us, *"Now faith is the substance of things hoped for, the evidence of things not seen."* I place my confidence in You, knowing that You are in control, and that You will move the mountains in my life for Your glory.

I thank You for the example of the centurion in **Matthew 8:10 NKJV**, whose great faith amazed Jesus. Father, I pray that my faith, too, would be great in Your sight. Help me to believe without hesitation, knowing that with You, all things are possible. I declare that no mountain will stand in my way as I walk forward in faith with You.

I commit today, Lord, to walk by faith and not by sight, as instructed in **2 Corinthians 5:7 NKJV**. I will not be swayed by what I see or feel but will move forward confidently in the promises You have made. I trust that You are faithful to complete the good work You have begun in me, as Philippians 1:6 assures us.

Finally, I stand on the powerful promise of **Romans 8:37 NKJV,** which tells us, *"Yet in all these things we are more than conquerors through Him who loved us."* Through Your love, Lord, I am more than a conqueror. Whatever mountains rise before me, I know that Your power will enable me to overcome them, and my faith will remain unshaken.

Thank You, Lord, for the precious gift of faith. I believe that You are at work in my life, moving mountains, opening doors, and making a way where there seems to be no way. I trust in Your power and Your promises, knowing that with You, all things are possible.

In the mighty name of Jesus, I pray. Amen.

CHAPTER SIX
FAITH AMIDST SUFFERING

An unavoidable aspect of being human is suffering. It might show up as anything from financial difficulties to emotional misery to physical pain to the devastating loss of a loved one. It is normal to struggle with important issues in the face of such hardship: Why must we go through pain? In times of suffering, where is God? How do we maintain our faith when life seems too much to handle?

Throughout this chapter, we will explore the profound reality that faith may not only endure suffering but thrive in it. Jesus Himself recognized the existence of adversity when He said to His disciples, *"These things I have spoken to you, that in Me you may have peace. In the world you will have tribulation; but be of good cheer, I have overcome the world."* But be encouraged! The world is above me **John 16:33 NKJV.** In the face of suffering, having faith does not imply that pain does not exist or that its significance should be lessened. Instead, it is the steadfast conviction that God is with us at our darkest moments, providing His courage, consolation, and promise that He will guide us through the storm so that we come out of it stronger, wiser, and closer to Him.

We will learn how faith may support us through difficult circumstances via biblical tales, inspirational verses, and firsthand accounts of tenacity. We'll look at why God permits suffering and how we might use our hardships to get closer to Him. The main emphasis will be on seeing that God is at work, molding us, developing our character, and setting us up for bigger goals in His plan—even in the midst of our worst pain. These times demonstrate the genuine profundity and tenacity of unshakable faith.

While suffering may defy human understanding, with faith, we can find peace in the midst of chaos. We can trust that our pain is never in vain, knowing that God has the power to redeem it, using it for both His glory and our good.

FINDING GOD IN PAIN AND LOSS

In the human experience, suffering is one of the most profound and difficult things. Suffering can feel pointless and lonely, whether it takes the form of physical pain, the intense anguish of losing a loved one, the sting of rejection, or the melancholy of spiritual despair. It is simple to wonder where God is in the middle of our suffering and to ask what the purpose of it is. A very different view of suffering, however, is provided by the Bible, which exhorts us to seek God not in spite of but frequently because of our suffering.

The prophet **Isaiah 53:3 NKJV** predicted that the Messiah would be *"a man of sorrows"* and *"acquainted with grief."* The suffering of the world did not spare Jesus, the Son of God, as this verse poignantly reminds us. He went through anguish, grief, and rejection as someone who really understood the breadth of human suffering rather than as an outsider. In addition to our bodily suffering, Jesus also bore the weight of our sin and grief.

Since we are not alone in our suffering, this truth gives us solace. Being human, Jesus is able to empathize with our deepest suffering. We are reminded of this in **Hebrews 4:15 NKJV**, where Jesus, our high priest *"For we do not have a High Priest who cannot sympathize with our weaknesses, but was in all points tempted as we are, yet without sin."* Jesus is not uncaring or unaffected by our difficulties. He offers His grace and empathy while walking with us through our pain.

Seeking quick answers to the **"why"** of our grief is not the goal of discovering God in the midst of suffering and loss. It involves discovering how to look for God's presence even when the causes of our suffering are unknown. We may never fully comprehend the reason for our pain on this side of eternity in many cases. But we are urged to have faith in the assurance of God's closeness. The assurance found in **Deuteronomy 31:6 NKJV** is that *"Be strong and of good courage, do not fear nor be afraid of them; for the Lord your God, He is the One who goes with you. He will not leave you nor forsake you."* This guarantee acts as a continual reminder that, even at our lowest moments, God's presence is a source of courage and hope.

Psalm 34:18 NKJV, which reads, *"The Lord is near to those who have a broken heart and saves such as have a contrite spirit."* further highlights God's personal concern for the suffering. We frequently discover that God is closer than we think when we are in the midst of our suffering. Although suffering can cause us to reflect, it can also bring us closer to the One who is sympathetic to our plight and provides consolation.

The story of Job in the Bible offers a profound example of faith amid unrelenting suffering. Job, a man of great wealth and righteousness, faced a devastating series of losses—his health, his wealth, and his family. In the face of this unimaginable suffering, Job's response was not one of despair or denial, but rather an unshakable trust in God's sovereignty.

He proclaimed, *"Though He slay me, yet will I trust Him. Even so, I will defend my own ways before Him."* **Job 13:15 NKJV.** Job's declaration was not rooted in blind faith, but in a deep, unwavering trust in the goodness and faithfulness of God. Even though he did not understand the reasons for his suffering, Job chose to rely on God's character, which he knew to be trustworthy and loving.

We can choose to believe in God's bigger plan even if we might not always know the precise causes of our suffering, as Job's example shows us. It is never pointless for us to endure. We might be shaped into the individuals God has called us to be as a result of it. God frequently uses hardship to pull us nearer to Himself, strengthening our confidence and reliance on His power.

Faith in the midst of pain does not require us to have all the answers, nor does it demand that we immediately *"feel better"* in the face of loss. It calls us to believe that, even in the most painful circumstances, God is present, working, and ultimately for our good.

The Apostle Paul writes in **2 Corinthians 1:3-4 NKJV** that God is *the "Blessed be the God and Father of our Lord Jesus Christ, the Father of mercies and God of all comfort, who comforts us in all our tribulation, that we may be able to comfort those who are in any trouble, with the comfort with which we ourselves are comforted by God."* Through our own experiences of suffering and loss, God equips us to be vessels of comfort to others, allowing us to offer empathy and hope to those in need.

Realizing that suffering is not a singular experience but rather a call to get closer to God is the first step toward discovering God in suffering and loss. We frequently experience the depth of His love and fidelity via our suffering. While we may not fully grasp the "why" of our suffering, we may rely in the "who" of our faith—the God who is there, who understands, and who promises to bring redemption even out of our darkest wounds

HOW UNSHAKABLE FAITH ENDURES THROUGH SUFFERING

Unshakable faith does not mean an absence of suffering; rather, it signifies the presence of a profound, unwavering trust in God, even in the midst of our deepest trials. It is the kind of faith that holds firm in the face of hardship, believing that our present struggles are not the final chapter in our story.

The apostle James encourages us in this truth in **James 1:2-4 NKJV,** saying, *"My brethren, count it all joy when you fall into various trials, knowing that the testing of your faith produces patience. But let patience have its perfect work, that you may be perfect and complete, lacking nothing."* James teaches us that faith, when tested by hardship, becomes more resilient and refined, leading us to spiritual maturity and a deeper relationship with God.

Faith that endures through suffering is not developed in moments of comfort or ease. It is forged in the fires of adversity. It is in the midst of our struggles that we are forced to shift our reliance from our own strength to God's limitless power.

In **Romans 5:3-5 NKJV,** Paul provides further insight into this process, writing, *"And not only that, but we also glory in tribulations, knowing that tribulation produces perseverance; and perseverance, character; and character, hope. Now hope does not disappoint, because the love of God has been poured out in our hearts by the Holy Spirit who was given to us."*

The apostle Paul, who himself endured extreme hardship for the sake of the gospel, offers a vivid illustration of enduring faith. In **2 Corinthians 4:8-9 NKJV,** Paul writes, *"We are hard-pressed on every side, yet not crushed; we are perplexed, but not in despair; persecuted, but not forsaken; struck down, but not destroyed."* Paul experienced numerous trials—shipwrecks, imprisonments, beatings, and countless other hardships—yet his faith remained unshaken.

His resilience was not based on his circumstances but on the **hope,** he found in Christ. Paul's faith teaches us that when we place our trust in Jesus, we can endure even the most difficult trials, for our hope is anchored in Him, not in our temporary circumstances.

The book of Hebrews, often called the *"faith hall of fame,"* offers a powerful testimony of those who demonstrated unshakable faith despite intense suffering. In Hebrews 11, we read about people who were persecuted, imprisoned, and even martyred for their faith. Yet, they did not turn away from God. Their faith was steadfast because they understood that their earthly struggles were temporary, but the reward that awaited them was eternal.

Unshakable faith accepts the suffering and difficulties of life but chooses to trust that God is greater than any hardship we encounter. It does not deny the existence of suffering. It is the knowledge that God's ultimate plan for our lives is certain, even if we do not fully comprehend the reasons behind our suffering.

This religion firmly believes that God will turn our pain into something positive in His perfect time, redeeming it and using it for His glory. Those who love God and have been called in accordance with His purpose benefit from everything that He does, as **Romans 8:28 NKJV** reminds us.

Moreover, unshakable faith provides us with the strength to endure not only for our own benefit but also for the sake of others. Our ability to endure suffering with hope and joy becomes a testimony to the world of God's faithfulness.

In **2 Corinthians 1:3-4 NKJV**, Paul writes, *"Blessed be the God and Father of our Lord Jesus Christ, the Father of mercies and God of all comfort, who comforts us in all our tribulation, that we may be able to comfort those who are in any trouble, with the comfort with which we ourselves are comforted by God."* Through our own experiences of suffering, God equips us to offer comfort and encouragement to others who are facing similar struggles.

Unshakeable faith is about finding purpose, optimism, and strength in suffering rather than avoiding it. Because it is based on God's unwavering character and His promises, it is a faith that endures. Because of this faith, we are able to endure hardships because we have faith that God is constantly working to improve us and get us ready for His bigger plans. Even if we experience hardship along the way, we may be sure that God's love will keep us going and that we shall emerge from it stronger and more completely changed.

THE HEALING POWER OF FAITH IN JESUS CHRIST

The amazing ability of faith to cure not just physically but also emotionally and spiritually is among its most profound truths. More than only sin forgiveness is provided by faith in Jesus Christ; it also heals our brokenness, restores our souls, and gives us the fortitude to face life's challenges. Jesus is the ultimate Healer who heals the deepest wounds in our hearts and souls in addition to being our Savior who saves us.

In **Matthew 11:28-30 NKJV**, Jesus extends an invitation that offers rest and peace amidst life's burdens: *"Come to Me, all you who labor and are heavy laden, and I will give you rest. Take My yoke upon you and learn from Me, for I am gentle and lowly in heart, and you will find rest for your souls. For My yoke is easy and My burden is light."*

Even in the midst of sorrow, this promise demonstrates the healing power of faith by providing a tranquility that is beyond human comprehension. Jesus provides us with both physical and spiritual relief when we confide in Him about our suffering and weariness.

Luke 8:43–48 NKJV tells the account of the woman with the blood problem, which vividly exemplifies the healing power of faith. This woman had been bleeding for twelve long years, wasting all her money on unsuccessful therapies. However, she was certain that Jesus had the ability to heal and that she would be restored simply by touching the hem of His garment. Her belief that Jesus could heal her in spite of years of pain prompted Jesus to act. *"Your faith has made you well. Go in peace,"* he murmured, turning to face her. In addition to mending physical illnesses, this experience shows how trust in Jesus can cure spiritual and emotional wounds. The woman was fully restored as a result of her confidence in Jesus' healing ability, serving as a potent reminder that having faith in Christ restores wholeness in all facets of our life.

Another compelling example of healing through faith is the story of the blind man in **John 9:1-12 NKJV**. When Jesus and His disciples came across a man who had been blind from birth, they questioned whether his blindness was a consequence of his own sin or that of his parents. Jesus clarified that neither was to blame; instead, the man's blindness was an opportunity for God's works to be revealed. Jesus healed the man, restoring his sight, and the man's faith led him to worship and believe in Jesus as the Son of God.

This story emphasizes how God may use pain as a means of displaying His might and glory rather than as a kind of punishment. The guy experienced the transforming power of faith in Jesus, which resulted in both spiritual and emotional restoration, in addition to bodily healing.

Jesus' healing power extends far beyond physical afflictions. He is the Healer of broken hearts, crushed spirits, and wounded souls. **Psalms 147:3 NKJV** affirms this, saying, *"He heals the brokenhearted and binds up their wounds."* No matter the type of suffering we endure, Jesus offers His healing touch, pouring out His love, grace, and peace into the deepest parts of our being. Whether we are battling depression, grief, or anxiety, the healing that Jesus provides is not just a temporary fix—it is a profound transformation that restores our emotional and spiritual well-being.

The healing power of Jesus enables us to discover peace and hope in the midst of emotional pain. His love has the power to restore what has been damaged, bringing light into our darkest hours and beauty out of ashes. Faith-based healing entails letting go of our suffering and letting God's presence provide solace and healing. By putting our faith in Jesus, we give ourselves over to His transformational power, which not only heals our bodies but also our minds and hearts.

Jesus' healing is a broad process, touching all area of our suffering—whether physical, emotional, or spiritual. When we accept His invitation to bring our troubles to Him, we discover a serenity that surpasses our current situation. We encounter a healing that goes well beyond simple physical recovery as we get closer to Him in faith.

Knowing that Jesus' healing touch is always available to us in times of need gives us the ability to face our struggles with joy and hope because He cures us from the inside out.

Faith in Jesus Christ has a transformative healing power that reaches deep into our hearts and souls, healing beyond our physical pain. Faith invites us to experience a peace and restoration that only Jesus can offer, one that heals brokenness, restores hope, and gives us the strength to keep going. When we trust in Jesus Christ, we open ourselves to the limitless healing power of His love and we start to experience the fullness of life He has promised.

A PERSONAL TESTIMONY OF FAITH IN THE MIDST OF SUFFERING: MY MOTHER'S DEATH

In July 2017, my life took an unexpected and devastating turn with a single phone call from my sister. She broke the heartbreaking news—our mother, who was in the Philippines at the time, had suffered a severe stroke. The distance between us magnified my fear and helplessness. I was thousands of miles away, unable to rush to her side or offer immediate comfort.

The news hit me like a thunderclap, shaking me to my core. My mind raced with questions: *Was she in pain? Was she receiving the care she needed? Would I ever hear her voice again?* The vivid image of her vibrant presence, now replaced by uncertainty, haunted me. The weight of being so far away in such a critical moment was unbearable.

In that instant, my world stood still, forever marked by the gravity of that phone call. The days that followed were a whirlwind of worry, prayers, and desperate attempts to stay connected despite the miles that separated us.

Yet, even in the depths of my despair, one thing remained unshaken: my faith. Despite the overwhelming odds, a quiet resolve took root in my heart, and I refused to give in to hopelessness, convinced that no situation was too dire for God's intervention, no mountain was too big for Him to move, and I clung to God's promises, believing that His healing power could perform miracles beyond human comprehension.

I leaned to prayer as my lifeline during that trying time, finding comfort in it. **James 5:16 NKJV**, which states that *"Confess your trespasses to one another, and pray for one another, that you may be healed. The effective, fervent prayer of a righteous man avails much."* struck a deep chord with me. My mother's healing was something I begged God for with all the enthusiasm I could muster. I also made an effort to connect with our church community, asking them to join me in prayer and to stand with me in faith. We joined our hearts in the belief that God's might could do something remarkable. No matter how lengthy and uncertain the days seemed, I never lost faith in His capacity to heal.

In the middle of the storm, hope became my rock. I waited expectantly with strong confidence, certain that a miracle was possible. I held fast to the conviction that God's hand was at work in the background, even though the proof was not yet visible.

I was sitting quietly at home one Wednesday morning when my pastor's daughter sent me an email, *"Our pastor would offer prayers for your mother at the evening service today"*. She said something that gave me a fresh sense of hope. My heart was full of anticipation as I attended the service with the hope that God would step in.

As the worship began, I stood amidst the congregation, tears cascading down my face. My soul poured out in raw, fervent cries to God. I fervently longed for His miracle touch because I firmly thought that He could cure my mother. I felt the unwavering certainty that I was not alone in my request as my faith and my desire merged at that precise moment.

Then, something happened that I could never have anticipated. In the middle of the sermon, our pastor suddenly stopped, muted his microphone, and descended from the stage. Confusion washed over me, but my heart also quickened with anticipation. As he approached me, he gently took my hand and said, *"God spoke to me tonight. Your mom is in God's hands."*

Tears welled in my eyes, and I whispered through my sobs, *"Yes, Pastor, I believe God will heal her."* But he looked at me with compassion and repeated, *"Listen to me. Your mom is in God's hands."* As if the very breath of God had spoken through him, his words stuck in my heart after he returned to the stage. Even though I wasn't entirely sure what he meant at the time, I felt a calmness that I couldn't quite put my finger on.

The service continued, and when it concluded, I received a phone call from my sisters. Their voices trembled with emotion as they shared the devastating news that our mother had passed away. In that moment, my heart broke—but something incredible happened within me. Rather than being overwhelmed by sorrow or anger, a profound peace flooded my soul. I realized, in that instant, that my mother was no longer in that hospital bed but was now in the presence of the Lord. As **2 Corinthians 5:8 NKJV** reminds us, *"We are confident, yes, well pleased rather to be absent from the body and to be present with the Lord."*

Despite the depth of my loss, I had an unexplainable sensation of calm that defied comprehension. It seemed as if God had softly readied my heart for this occasion, enveloping me in a solace that only He could offer. I thought of my pastor's comforting statement, "Your mom is in God's hands." Clinging to this truth, I shared it with my sisters, and in that sacred moment of loss, something extraordinary happened.

Our sorrow, though genuine, began to shift. My tears no longer fell from a place of despair but from a wellspring of joy and gratitude. I knew, beyond any doubt, that my mother was now resting in the loving embrace of God.

Even when His plan seemed inconceivable, I could feel the weight of His presence almost physically, as though He were holding me and whispering to my spirit that it was flawless. I sought safety in His enormous and immense love, which transformed my sorrow into a deep sense of optimism.

In the middle of my sorrow, I came to see that this loss was not the end but rather the start of something lovely—a more profound and personal comprehension of God's faithfulness and love. His calm, which is beyond comprehension, surrounded me in a manner I could never have predicted. I begged for healing, but God, in His omniscience, provided a far better answer than I could have ever imagined. The real miracle had been His love, and I had found His embrace in my sorrow.

I want to encourage everyone who is experiencing grief, loss, or uncertainty to cling to the belief that God's love is unwavering. His intentions are bigger than our comprehension, and His ways are superior than ours. He is there at the darkest times, providing unfailing love and a calm that surpasses sorrow. Deep down, I've realized that God's love is what gives us the strength to continue, even while we're grieving, and that it really does move mountains.

Conclusion

A natural aspect of the human experience is suffering. Dealing with physical discomfort, mental distress, or the weight of loss can be overwhelming and isolating. Faith gives us the fortitude to persevere and reassures us that we are never alone, even in the midst of our most intense suffering. Even while we might not always comprehend the causes of our pain, faith serves as a reminder that God is real and is at work in ways that are beyond our comprehension.

Unshakable faith adheres to God in the face of uncertainty rather than avoiding adversity. Believing that God is with us through every hardship and that our suffering has a higher purpose—both for His glory and our eventual good—is a trust that survives even in the darkest moments. We can find serenity in the knowledge that pain has purpose when we cling to this unwavering faith. Rather, it turns into a conduit for the manifestation of God's power, love, and healing.

Faith in Jesus Christ is the key that opens the door to divine healing. His power to heal is not limited to physical ailments; it extends to emotional wounds, spiritual struggles, and the brokenness of the human soul. No matter the size or scope of our suffering, Jesus' healing power knows no bounds. He does not simply meet us at our point of need, but goes beyond that, bringing restoration and wholeness to all aspects of our lives. His invitation to come to Him in times of pain reassures us that He will never leave us or forsake us.

Even when the burden of suffering feels unbearable, we can hold fast to the truth that God is present with us, that He cares for us, and that His love will sustain us through it all. Jesus, the *"Man of Sorrows"* who endured the deepest forms of human suffering, walks with us through every trial we encounter. He understands our pain not from a distant viewpoint, but from His own personal experience. In Him, we encounter a compassionate Savior who offers more than just comfort—He offers profound and transformative healing.

As you face your own struggles, remember that you are never alone. The presence of Jesus, who bore our griefs and carried our sorrows, is with you every step of the way. His healing touch is available to bring peace where there is chaos, strength where there is weakness, and hope where there is despair. No storm is too fierce, no wound too deep, for His love and power to heal. By keeping your faith firmly anchored in Him, you will find that no matter how intense the pain may be, His grace is sufficient, and His power is perfected in our weakness.

The ability of faith to heal does not guarantee that pain will cease, but it does reassure us that suffering can be redeemed via Christ. Faith becomes the means by which we become nearer to God, learn about His faithfulness, and experience His life-changing activity. We can have unwavering faith that God will eventually bring about healing, restoration, and a restored sense of strength for both the present and the future He is planning.

A PRAYER FOR STRENGTH AND FAITH AMIDST SUFFERING

Heavenly Father,

I come before You today, heavy with the burden of my suffering, seeking Your presence and comfort. Your Word assures me that You are near to the brokenhearted and that You heal those who are crushed in spirit **Psalm 34:18 NKJV.** In these moments of pain, I place my trust in Your promises, knowing that You Walk beside me every step of the way.

In **2 Corinthians 1:3-4 NKJV,** Your Word tells us, *"Blessed be the God and Father of our Lord Jesus Christ, the Father of mercies and God of all comfort, who comforts us in all our tribulation, that we may be able to comfort those who are in any trouble, with the comfort with which we ourselves are comforted by God."* I thank You, Lord, for being the God of all comfort. Wrap me in Your loving arms today, fill my heart with Your peace, and bring healing to my soul through Your presence.

When facing trials, I cling to the truth of **Romans 8:18 NKJV,** which says, *"For I consider that the sufferings of this present time are not worthy to be compared with the glory which shall be revealed in us."* Father, though the pain feels overwhelming, I know it is temporary. You are preparing something far greater, and I trust that You are working all things together for my good Romans 8:28.

Lord, Your Word in **James 1:2-4 NKJV** says, *"My brethren, count it all joy when you fall into various trials, knowing that the testing of your faith produces patience. But let patience have its perfect work, that you may be perfect and complete, lacking nothing."* I pray that through this trial, You would strengthen my faith. Help me find joy even in the struggle, knowing that You are using this time to refine me, make me more like You, and build endurance in my life.

In **Isaiah 43:2 NKJV**, You promise, *"When you pass through the waters, I will be with you; And through the rivers, they shall not overflow you. When you walk through the fire, you shall not be burned, nor shall the flame scorch you."* Lord, I hold on to this promise today. I trust that even in the deepest waters and fiercest flames, You are with me, protecting me, and guiding me through. I will not be consumed by my suffering because You are with me every step of the way.

Father, I remember the words of **1 Peter 5:10 NKJV**, *"But may the God of all grace, who called us to His eternal glory by Christ Jesus, after you have suffered a while, perfect, establish, strengthen, and settle you."* I claim this promise of restoration. Though I am in pain now, I trust that You will heal, strengthen, and establish me.

Even in my suffering, I choose to follow the example of Jesus, who endured the cross for the joy set before Him. Lord, grant me the strength to endure, to fix my eyes on You, and to trust that Your purposes are greater than any pain I may feel.

Father, help me to remember that **2 Corinthians 4:17 NKJV** says, *"For our light affliction, which is but for a moment, is working for us a far more exceeding and eternal weight of glory."* I know this suffering is temporary, and that You are preparing me for a glory that will surpass all my trials.

Lord, I surrender my pain to You. I trust You in the midst of my suffering, knowing that You are working all things for my good and Your glory. I believe in Your power to heal, restore, and strengthen me, and I place my hope fully in You. Thank You for being my refuge, my strength, and my ever-present help in times of trouble **Psalm 46:1 NKJV.** In Jesus' name, I pray. ***Amen.***

CHAPTER SEVEN
THE FRUIT OF UNSHAKABLE FAITH

Faith is an active, transformational force that shapes us and produces observable results in our lives; it is not just a passive idea we have in our hearts. Strong faith flourishes in our deep relationship with God, producing long-lasting and significant effects, much like a tree that feeds from its roots buried deep in fertile soil to bear fruit.

Our unshakable faith in Jesus Christ becomes a pillar as we face life's obstacles and rejoice in its joys, molding our personalities, enhancing our relationships, and spurring social change.

We'll concentrate on the amazing transformation that unwavering faith brings about in our lives. The fruit of the Spirit is produced as our faith starts to mold us into the likeness of Christ as our relationship with God grows stronger. Paul enumerates the following qualities of this type of faith in **Galatians 5:22–23 NKJV**: love, joy, peace, longsuffering, kindness, goodness, faithfulness, gentleness, and self-control. These characteristics arise naturally from a life that is given over to God and guided by the Holy Spirit; they are not merely attributes to aspire to.

This fruit is not something we can generate on our own. It is the result of the Holy Spirit working within us, as we stay rooted in Christ and trust His guidance. Just as a healthy tree naturally produces fruit when nourished, a life anchored in Christ will naturally bear fruit that blesses others and glorifies God.

In examining the fruit of our faith, we are called to evaluate the way our lives reflect Christ's character. When our faith is unshakable, it is evident not only in our own transformation but also in the way we impact others and bring light into the world. The fruit of unshakable faith is not just a personal blessing but a witness to others of God's love, grace, and power.

This chapter will discuss the transformational fruit that results from developing and fostering our faith in God. According to the Bible, faith is an active trust in God's promises, character, and capacity to move and work in our lives rather than just a belief in His existence. This type of faith is neither inactive nor inert; it bears fruit that embodies Christ's essence, exalting God and furthering His kingdom.

As we progress through this chapter, we will consider how unwavering faith might transform a believer's life. We'll examine biblical accounts of people who showed unshakeable faith and the significant influence their faith had on their own and others' lives. Additionally, we will present firsthand accounts of how faith has impacted people's lives, offering tangible proof of the benefits that result from a strong, unwavering relationship with God.

This chapter also invites us to examine the outcomes of our religion. Do our deeds reflect the religion we profess to hold? Does our faith give us the compassion, kindness, and tolerance that define Christ's heart for others? Does it inspire those around us to seek a deeper relationship with Him? The fruit of unwavering faith is evidence of God's activity in our lives and shows that we are doing what He has commanded and accomplishing His goals.

Let us reflect on what it means to live a life that bears the fruit of true, unshakable faith—one that continually draws us closer to God, reflects His nature, and brings hope and healing to the world. By nurturing our faith, we align ourselves with God's will and become instruments of His love and purpose in the world around us.

HOW FAITH LEADS TO PEACE, JOY, AND PURPOSE

Unshakable faith produces tangible, transformative results that flow from a deep, unwavering trust in God. True faith is more than just intellectual assent to the existence of God or an acknowledgment of theological truths—it is an active reliance on His promises, His goodness, and His sovereignty in every aspect of our lives. This kind of faith nurtures peace, joy, and purpose, regardless of the challenges we encounter.

In **Philippians 4:6-7 NKJV,** the Apostle Paul encourages believers, saying, *"Be anxious for nothing, but in everything by prayer and supplication, with thanksgiving, let your requests be made known to God; and the peace of*

God, which surpasses all understanding, will guard your hearts and minds through Christ Jesus."

Here, Paul underscores a profound truth: peace is the direct outcome of placing our faith in God. While the world may offer temporary and fragile moments of peace, the peace that God provides is enduring and surpasses all human understanding. This serenity, which is independent of favorable circumstances, is based on our belief in God's sovereignty and control over all occurrences.

During difficult, uncertain, or stormy times, this divine serenity—which comes from a steadfast faith in Christ—serves as a shield to protect our hearts and minds.

In addition to peace, joy is another vital fruit that grows from a life grounded in unshakable faith. However, this joy is not dependent on our external circumstances; rather, it is a deep, inner contentment that comes from knowing we are loved, secure in God's presence, and confident in His ultimate control over our lives.

In **Romans 15:13 NKJV**, Paul prays, *"Now may the God of hope fill you with all joy and peace in believing, that you may abound in hope by the power of the Holy Spirit."* Joy, in this sense, is a byproduct of trusting in God's faithful character.

As we place our trust in Him, we experience not only joy and peace but also an overflowing hope—hope that carries us forward even in the face of challenges or uncertainty. This hope serves as a powerful motivator and anchor, providing strength and encouragement throughout life's trials.

Equally significant is the sense of purpose that emerges from a life of unshakable faith. When we anchor our lives in faith, we are grounded in the truth that our existence holds meaning and that we are part of God's greater plan. In **Jeremiah 29:11 NKJV**, God assures His people *"For I know the thoughts that I think toward you, says the Lord, thoughts of peace and not of evil, to give you a future and a hope."* This promise reminds us that God's sovereignty extends to every aspect of our lives.

We can trust in His plan and know that He is guiding our steps even when the path is unclear or difficult. We may move forward with security because we have guidance and confidence knowing that we are a part of His divine purpose. No matter what challenges we face, we have the courage to follow our mission because we know that God is steadfastly leading us toward a bright future.

Unwavering faith actively fosters serenity, happiness, and a strong sense of purpose in addition to helping us get through life's challenges. Our hearts are stabilized by these fruits of faith, which enable us to face life's challenges with assurance and optimism.

Faith in God's goodness and sovereignty leads to a deep understanding of our role in God's divine plan, an inner delight that outweighs all other emotions, and lasting peace. When we trust in Him, we discover that these blessings of happiness, serenity, and purpose are not fleeting but rather the outcome of living a life founded on God's steadfast love and faithfulness.

Building a Life of Hope and Confidence

Living a life grounded in unwavering faith goes far beyond simply feeling moments of peace or joy. It is about cultivating a life marked by unyielding hope and profound confidence, even when the future appears uncertain and the path ahead unclear. Such faith does not retreat in the face of fear or doubt, but instead pushes forward with the firm assurance that God is trustworthy and will fulfill His promises, regardless of current circumstances.

In **Romans 8:28 NKJV,** we are reminded of a powerful truth: *"And we know that all things work together for good to those who love God, to those who are the called according to His purpose."* The scripture is a pillar of hope, assuring us that God is constantly working in the background of every situation in our lives. We can be confident that He is perfectly arranging everything for our good and His glory, even when we cannot see His hand at work. Because we have faith in God's divine purpose and His unwavering devotion to us, this reality gives us a solid foundation of confidence even in times of ambiguity and difficulty.

Moreover, unshakable faith fosters a bold, courageous confidence in God's ability to accomplish the impossible. In **Matthew 17:20 NKJV**, Jesus assures His followers, *"So Jesus said to them, 'Because of your unbelief; for assuredly, I say to you, if you have faith as a mustard seed, you will say to this* *mountain, "Move from here to there," and it will move; and nothing will be impossible for you."* This emphasizes that the power of faith does not lie in the quantity of belief, but in its object—the all-powerful, sovereign Creator.

When we place our faith in God, we gain the confidence that He is capable of performing the extraordinary, from moving mountains to opening doors that seemed forever shut. In Him, the impossible becomes possible, and the future, though unknown, is filled with infinite potential.

The Bible is filled with tales of people who, despite seemingly insurmountable obstacles, lived lives full of courage and hope by establishing their lives on this unwavering foundation of faith. We see examples of men and women who, by placing their confidence in God, overcame adversity, endured hardships, and saw God's promises come to pass—from the patriarchs of the Old Testament to the apostles of the New Testament.

Take, for example, the story of Abraham, who, despite his old age and the barrenness of his wife Sarah, held fast to God's promise of descendants as numerous as the stars. His faith never wavered, and as a result, God blessed him with a son, Isaac, and through him, a great nation. This kind of faith is not blind optimism; it is a deep, rooted trust that God's promises are not dependent on our circumstances but on His unchanging nature.

Similarly, the Apostle Paul exemplified this kind of steadfast faith throughout his life. Despite facing imprisonment, shipwrecks, and constant persecution, Paul never faltered in his confidence that God's plan for him was good and purposeful. His life is a testament to the power of unshakable faith—a faith that transforms fear into courage and doubt into unwavering conviction.

Developing a strong, unwavering faith in God is the first step towards creating a life of hope and confidence in our own lives. It is making the decision to put our faith in Him, even in the face of uncertainty, and having the guts to think that He is working in every circumstance, creating His ideal plan for our lives.

As we develop this faith, we will find that confidence and optimism begin to permeate every aspect of our lives, enabling us to face challenges head-on and savor every moment. Because we have trust that our Heavenly Father will always be there to guide us, we not only survive life's storms but thrive.

LIVING A TESTIMONY OF FAITH

One of the most profound and impactful fruits of unshakable faith is its ability to serve as a testimony to others. Our faith is not something meant to be kept in silence or obscurity; it is designed to be lived out openly, to shine brightly as a beacon of hope, encouragement, and divine truth to those around us. When we choose to live by faith, our lives become living reflections of God's power, faithfulness, and transformative love.

Jesus exhorts His disciples to shine their light on the world by declaring, *"You are the light of the world. A city that is set on a hill cannot be hidden. Nor do they light a lamp and put it under a basket, but on a lampstand, and it gives light to all who are in the house. Let your light so shine before men, that they may see your good works and glorify your Father in heaven."* in **Matthew 5:14–16 NKJV.**

It is impossible to conceal a town situated atop a hill. People also don't light a lamp and place it beneath a bowl. Rather, they place it on its stand, which illuminates the entire house. Shine your light in a similar manner so that others can see your good deeds and glorify your heavenly Father. Jesus emphasizes that rather than being hidden, our faith should be open and obvious.

Others are exposed to the truth of God's goodness and power through the outward manifestations of our faith—our words, deeds, and attitudes. Our lives are meant to draw others to the light of Christ, pointing them toward the hope and truth found in Him.

A powerful way to live out our faith and provide a testimony to others is by embodying the fruit of the Spirit, as outlined in **Galatians 5:22-23 NKJV**: *"But the fruit of the Spirit is love, joy, peace, longsuffering, kindness, goodness, faithfulness, gentleness, self-control. Against such there is no law."*

These qualities are not just characteristics to aspire to—they are the natural outpouring of a life surrendered to God's Spirit. When we walk in step with the Spirit, our actions speak volumes about the reality of our faith. The world notices when we respond with love instead of anger, joy in the middle of sorrow, kindness in a cruel and divided world, and peace in times of turmoil. These fruits not only transform our own lives but also serve as a powerful example of God's benevolence and might.

Furthermore, living a testimony of faith means being ready to share the reason for the hope we possess. **1 Peter 3:15 NKJV** encourages believers *"But sanctify the Lord God in your hearts, and always be ready to give a defense to everyone who asks you a reason for the hope that is in you, with meekness and fear."* People will naturally want to know where our joy, tranquility, and unshakable hope originate from as we live our lives with unwavering faith.

When we remain steadfast in our faith throughout trying circumstances, it will be impossible to ignore the difference between our calm and the world's fear. The truth of Christ's love will be shown when we react to stressful situations with grace. Our faith-marked lives become a living testimony, allowing us to share the gospel's transformative power with others and inspiring them to ask where our optimism comes from.

Living a testimony of faith is not about perfection—it's about authenticity. It's about allowing God to work through us in our everyday actions and decisions, so that others can see His love, mercy, and grace at work. It's about letting our lives speak louder than our words, as we become walking testimonies of God's faithfulness. When we live with an unshakable faith, others will see the light of Christ in us, and they will be drawn to the source of our hope: the Savior who transforms lives and offers eternal life to all who believe.

Conclusion

Unshakable faith is far more than a theoretical concept or abstract belief—it is a dynamic, living force that produces tangible, real-world results in our lives. When we place our trust in God's promises and rely on His power, our faith has the capacity to transform us from the inside out. It becomes the foundation for lasting peace, guarding our hearts in times of turmoil; it produces a joy that strengthens us through all circumstances; and it imparts a sense of purpose that provides direction on our life's journey. True faith builds our confidence in God's ability to do the impossible, enabling us to face life's challenges with unwavering hope and trust.

As we grow in our faith and allow the Holy Spirit to work within us, we begin to display the fruit of the Spirit, which includes self-control, love, patience, kindness, and gentleness. These qualities not only assist in shaping our personalities but also show others how God's influence may change our lives. Our words, deeds, and attitudes demonstrate our faith and demonstrate the truth of God's grace at work within us.

Living out this kind of faith is not about achieving perfection—rather, it is about remaining rooted in Christ, trusting in His grace, and allowing His Spirit to guide and empower us. It is through this ongoing surrender to God's will that we produce fruit that blesses others, glorifies God, and points the world to the hope we have in Jesus Christ. Every fruit of faith we bear is a visible sign of God's presence and power in our lives, an invitation to others to experience His love and faithfulness.

Let your life be a living testimony of unshakable faith. Let it be a witness to the peace, joy, and purpose that only God can provide. And remember, each manifestation of faith in your life is a reflection of God's eternal presence and His unyielding commitment to guide you, strengthen you, and transform you.

A PRAYER FOR THE FRUIT OF UNSHAKABLE FAITH

Heavenly Father,

I come before You with a heart filled with gratitude for Your unwavering love and faithfulness. Thank You for the precious gift of faith, which You have graciously planted in my heart. As I continue this journey of faith, I humbly ask for Your help in bearing the fruit of unshakable faith in every area of my life. May Your presence and power shine brightly through me, so that others may see Your glory and be drawn closer to You.

Your Word in **Galatians 5:22-23 NKJV** teaches us that *"But the fruit of the Spirit is love, joy, peace, longsuffering, kindness, goodness, faithfulness, gentleness, self-control. Against such there is no law."*

Lord, I pray that the fruit of the Spirit would be evident in my life. May each of these qualities be cultivated within me through my unwavering trust in You. Strengthen me to grow in love, joy, peace, and all the fruits that arise from a heart deeply rooted in You.

In **John 15:5 NKJV**, Jesus declares, *"I am the vine, you are the branches. He who abides in Me, and I in him, bears much fruit; for without Me you can do nothing."* Father, I acknowledge that without You, I am nothing. I cannot bear any fruit apart from Your presence in my life. Today, I surrender myself to You, asking You to remain in me and empower me to bear abundant fruit. May Your Spirit dwell richly in me, transforming my heart and making me more like Christ each day.

Lord, I long to live a life of faith that reflects Your goodness. As You remind us in **Matthew 7:17 NKJV**, *"Even so, every good tree bears good fruit, but a bad tree bears bad fruit."* I ask that You prune away anything within me that does not honor You. Strengthen my faith so that my life may bear fruit that brings glory to Your name. May others see the evidence of Your work in me and be inspired to seek You.

In **Colossians 1:10 NKJV,** Your Word says, *"That you may walk worthy of the Lord, fully pleasing Him, being fruitful in every good work and increasing in the knowledge of God."* Father, I pray that my life would be a living testimony of Your goodness and that I would bear fruit in every good work I do. Help me to grow in the knowledge of You, that I may walk in a manner worthy of Your calling and reflect Your love and truth to the world.

I also hold fast to the promise found in **Psalms 1:3 NKJV,** *"He shall be like a tree planted by the rivers of water, that brings forth its fruit in its season, whose leaf also shall not wither; and whatever he does shall prosper."* Lord, plant me firmly by the streams of living water, Your Word, and nourish my soul with Your truth. Let my faith remain steadfast and fruitful, and may I prosper in the work You have called me to do.

As I continue to grow in faith, I embrace the truth of **Romans 15:13 NKJV,** which declares, *"Now may the God of hope fill you with all joy and peace in believing, that you may abound in hope by the power of the Holy Spirit."* Lord, fill me with joy and peace as I place my trust in You. May my faith overflow with hope, and may I bring hope to others through the power of Your Holy Spirit.

Father, I also acknowledge Your promise in **James 1:12 NKJV**, *"Blessed is the man who endures temptation; for when he has been approved, he will receive the crown of life which the Lord has promised to those who love Him."* Help me to remain faithful and steadfast through every trial. May I trust that these trials are refining me, producing righteousness and character, and drawing me closer to You. Let my unshakable faith be a reflection of Your glory and an example for others.

Lord, I thank You for the abundant life You offer to those who trust in You. I pray that my faith would bear lasting fruit, glorifying You in everything I do. May the fruit of my life reflect Your goodness, faithfulness, and love to the world around me.

In Jesus' name, I pray.

Amen.

CHAPTER EIGHT
HOW TO CULTIVATE UNSHAKABLE FAITH

Faith is a lifelong journey—a dynamic and always changing connection with God that develops, matures, and gets stronger over time—rather than merely a passing feeling or a single decision made in a flash. Our spiritual well-being takes deliberate attention and constant work, much like our physical health. Although unshakable faith is ultimately a gift from God, it also calls for our dedication to nurture and develop it.

Think of faith as a tender plant in a garden—it flourishes when we water it with prayer, nourish it with scripture, and shield it from the weeds of doubt and distraction. By actively tending to our faith, we ensure it remains steadfast and resilient, capable of weathering life's inevitable storms.

We will start by discussing the need of regular spiritual activities like church, prayer, and Bible reading as a basis for enhancing our faith. These exercises offer us a solid foundation in God's Word, remind us of His constant presence, and give us the fortitude to deal with life's challenges.

Regular worship and daily study of God's Word strengthen our hearts and enable us to consistently believe in His goodness and promises.

In addition to personal practices, the support and accountability found within a faith community play a vital role in strengthening our trust in God. As we gather with others who share in our journey, we encourage and uplift one another, creating an environment where faith can be nurtured.

The collective wisdom and shared experiences of fellow believers serve as reminders that we are not alone, even in the most trying moments. Together, we stand firm in our commitment to God, supporting one another in love and truth.

Developing solid faith also requires trusting God in all stages of life. It's important to understand that faith develops via both the challenges and hardships we encounter as well as during moments of joy and success. Indeed, difficulty and sorrow frequently serve to build and hone our faith. Our faith in God is strengthened by the difficulties we face, just like a metal is cleansed by fire.

These trying times provide us a chance to grow in our faith and become more dependent on God's power and control.

As we explore these principles and practices, we can draw inspiration from the countless examples of faith found in the Bible and in the lives of those around us. The testimonies of faithful men and women remind us that cultivating unshakable faith is not only possible but is the key to living a life filled with peace, joy, and purpose. Their journeys of faith show us that, through God's grace, it is possible to remain steadfast in the face of trials and to experience His presence in profound ways.

In this chapter, we will explore the practical steps necessary for cultivating a faith that remains unshaken, no matter what life may bring. Developing such a faith is neither simple nor instantaneous; it requires dedication, perseverance, and a deep reliance on God's grace. Through consistent effort, we can build a faith that endures and holds strong, regardless of the circumstances.

This chapter is a challenge to consciously develop an unwavering faith— a call to action. a faith that, rather than faltering in the face of hardship, gets stronger with each experience. We can establish a solid and unwavering foundation of faith by fostering our connection with God, depending on His Word, participating in a community of believers, and putting our trust in Him at all times. Together, let's set out on this adventure to discover ways to deepen our faith, honor God, and produce enduring fruit for His Kingdom.

DAILY PRACTICES TO STRENGTHEN YOUR FAITH

Like any genuine relationship, faith is a dynamic and ever-evolving process that calls for constant attention, intentionality, and work. Our relationship with God grows via everyday activities that purposefully foster our faith, just as a relationship with a close friend or family member does through consistent communication, mutual trust, and shared experiences. If we want to develop spiritually, our faith cannot be stagnant.

It must be cultivated and strengthened on a daily basis, much like physical fitness, which demands regular exercise to build, maintain, and enhance strength. Similarly, unshakable faith is developed through disciplined spiritual habits that are practiced consistently over time.

These activities, which are based on scripture, prayer, worship, and service, deepen our relationship with God, deepen our trust in His promises, and provide us with the courage to face life's inevitable challenges with hope and assurance. We can better comprehend God's character, will, and the promises He has given us by consistently studying His Word. By meditating and memorizing Scripture, we internalize the principles that uphold our faith, enabling them to serve as a solid foundation for us to rely on in difficult times.

Together, these daily practices form a spiritual discipline that equips us to navigate life's challenges with resilience and steadfastness. Just as an athlete's performance improves through regular training, so too does our faith grow stronger and more resilient through consistent spiritual practices.

As we commit ourselves to these habits, we are actively nurturing our relationship with God and positioning ourselves to receive His guidance, strength, and peace in every situation.

It is through deliberate, everyday actions that our faith becomes unwavering. Our faith in God grows when we consistently strive to get closer to Him and are reminded of His constancy. By doing this, we get the strength that God gives us to face each day with the assurance that we can overcome any challenges that may arise.

PRAYER: DEEPENING OUR CONNECTION WITH

Prayer is one of the most direct and intimate ways to communicate with God. It is foundational in nurturing our faith, as it aligns our hearts with God's will and keeps us attuned to His presence in our lives. Through prayer, we acknowledge God's sovereignty, express our dependence on Him, and reaffirm our trust in His ability to guide us through every circumstance.

In **Philippians 4:6-7 NKJV,** *"Be anxious for nothing, but in everything by prayer and supplication, with thanksgiving, let your requests be made known to God; and the peace of God, which surpasses all understanding, will guard your hearts and minds through Christ Jesus."* we are encouraged to bring our requests to God "with thanksgiving," and in turn, the peace of God will guard our hearts and minds. Prayer is not merely about asking for help but about developing a relationship with God in which we are reminded that we are never alone. It is through prayer that we come to understand that God is intimately involved in every aspect of our lives, which in turn strengthens our faith and fosters a deeper sense of peace and trust.

Scripture Reading: Immersing Ourselves in God's Truth

The Bible is the living Word of God, containing wisdom and revelation that illuminate our understanding of His character, His promises, and His plan for our lives. Regular reading and meditation on Scripture are vital for cultivating unshakable faith. As we immerse ourselves in God's Word, we constantly renew our minds and hearts, reminding ourselves of His truth, His faithfulness, and His unwavering love for us.

"So, then faith comes by hearing, and hearing by the word of God." according to **Romans 10:17 NKJV.** Because Scripture enables us to hear God's message clearly and fills our hearts with the knowledge of His promises and His unwavering faithfulness throughout history, it is one of the best ways to strengthen our faith. Every verse we read serves as a reminder that God is reliable, and as we absorb His Word, our faith and confidence in Him increase.

Worship: A Lifestyle of Reverence and Gratitude

Worship is more than just singing hymns or attending church services; it is a lifestyle that continually acknowledges and honors God's greatness and sovereignty in every area of our lives. Worship refocuses our hearts, shifting our attention away from our problems and placing it squarely on God's power, goodness, and majesty.

Psalms 95:6 NKJV invites us to, *"Oh come, let us worship and bow down; Let us kneel before the Lord our Maker."* Worship reminds us of God's greatness, reinforcing our reliance on Him. In worship, we are brought face to face with the reality that our faith stands on the immovable foundation of God's character and not on our current circumstances, and our hearts are filled with gratitude. Thanksgiving is a natural fruit of genuine worship and an important building block in the faith of a believer-especially as it relates to hardship. In addition to strengthening our bond with God, worshiping Him cultivates an attitude of thankfulness that sustains our faith throughout life's phases.

THE IMPORTANCE OF COMMUNITY AND SUPPORT IN FAITH

Shared Testimonies: A Source of Strength

One of the most powerful ways that community fosters unshakable faith is through the sharing of testimonies. When we hear the stories of how God has worked in the lives of others, it strengthens our own faith.

In **Revelation 12:11 NKJV,** it is written, *"And they overcame him by the blood of the Lamb and by the word of their testimony, and they did not love their lives to the death."* Testimonies not only remind others of His faithfulness but inspire and uplift in their spiritual journey as well. And when we tell our stories, we are able to help people in believing God's strength and promises as we give testimony to His changeless character and His ability to work in and through us.

Serving Together in Faith: Living Out God's Love

Serving others is another vital aspect of growing in faith. When we step out to serve in the name of Christ, we live out His love and experience His presence in tangible ways. Serving allows us to witness firsthand the impact of God's love on the lives of others, and it strengthens our own faith as we see God at work through our actions.

In **Matthew 25:40 NKJV,** Jesus reminds us *"And the King will answer and say to them, 'Assuredly, I say to you, inasmuch as you did it to one of the least of these My brethren, you did it to Me."* Serving in this way allows us to align our hearts with God's will, deepen our compassion, and grow in our understanding of His heart for others. Through service, we experience the power of God's love in action and are reminded of our calling to be the hands and feet of Christ in a hurting world.

STRENGTHENING FAITH THROUGH WORSHIP, FELLOWSHIP, AND SERVICE

While individual practices such as prayer, Bible study, and worship are essential to building a strong and lasting faith, the role of community—through fellowship, accountability, and shared service—cannot be overstated. Worshiping together strengthens our collective faith, while fellowship and accountability provide the encouragement and support necessary to navigate life's challenges. Sharing testimonies and serving others also plays a key role in deepening our faith as we witness God's power in action.

As we engage in these practices, we not only grow in our own faith but also contribute to the growth of others, creating a vibrant and supportive community that honors God and builds His Kingdom. Through the strength of fellowship, worship, and service, we cultivate a faith that is unshakable, enduring, and rooted in the love and promises of God.

A PERSONAL TESTIMONY OF CULTIVATING UNSHAKABLE FAITH

During some of the darkest seasons of my life, when I faced overwhelming adversity, I made a deliberate choice to not allow my circumstances to shake my faith in God. Rather than surrendering to despair or allowing fear to dictate my actions, I anchored myself in the promises of God and committed to living according to His will. In the face of trials, I chose to walk in righteousness and obedience, seeking His presence even in the most challenging moments.

Amid my struggles, I made worship a central part of my life, offering my heart to God in surrender and trust. I relinquished my burdens to Him, acknowledging that He was sovereign, even when I could not see the path ahead. As **Proverbs 3:5-6 NKJV** reminds us, *"Trust in the Lord with all your heart, and lean not on your own understanding; in all your ways acknowledge Him, and He shall direct your paths."*

By surrendering everything to God, I experienced a profound peace, a peace that transcended the understanding of my circumstances **Philippians 4:7 NKJV**. Trust is worshipping during difficulties, giving life totally to God, and on this premise, He founded His unshakable peace in my heart.

And so, I stood comforted in this thought that I was never alone while the howling storms of life raged around me. Despite being frightening, each trial served as a chance for God to show His faithfulness and strength in ways I could not have predicted.

His grace, through it all, somehow had me pressing on in moments when I could have given up. That's what **2 Corinthians 12:9 NKJV** reminds us: *"My grace is sufficient for you, for My strength is made perfect in weakness."* It was in the depth of my weakness that His strength shone bright, carrying me when I could no longer carry myself. These trials were to my spiritual benefit, refining-like fire-trying my faith and strengthening it to a foundation so unshakeable that nothing could destroy it.

Now, I stand firm, unshaken by the challenges life brings. Each difficulty I have faced has become a testimony to the strength of God's love and power, building a foundation of faith that remains unwavering. As David proclaimed in **Psalms 62:6 NKJV,** *"He only is my rock and my salvation; He is my defense; I shall not be moved."*

The adversities I have faced were not merely battles to overcome but stepping stones that have deepened my trust in God. Through them, I learned that true victory does not come from my own abilities but from the strength of the Lord. I can now echo Paul's words from **Romans 8:37 NKJV**: *"Yet in all these things we are more than conquerors through Him who loved us."*

God has used every adversity to sharpen me, deepen my faith, build my resilience, shape my character and show me that He is always there in my life. My faith is stronger today because I know that God will always be dependable. I stand confidently, knowing that He will guide me to triumph once more, no matter what obstacles the future may present.

Conclusion

The journey of cultivating unshakable faith is not a one-time event but a lifelong process. It demands dedication, persistence, and an intentional commitment to grow in our relationship with God and with others. By engaging in daily practices such as prayer, worship, Scripture reading, and fellowship, we create a strong foundation for a faith that remains steadfast in every circumstance.

Through these practices, we deepen our trust in God, and our faith becomes unshakable, capable of enduring even the most difficult trials. As we grow in our relationship with God, we not only strengthen ourselves but also become living testimonies of His faithfulness and power. Just as a tree's roots grow deep to withstand the fiercest storms, our faith deepens through God's

Word, prayer, and community, enabling us to stand firm no matter what life may throw our way.

Unwavering faith is a daily decision to believe God in everything; it is not about being perfect. As we continue to grow in this faith, we will reap fruits of peace, joy, and confidence, giving glory to God and changing the world. As we build our faith, we are ready to fulfill God's purpose for our life and expand His Kingdom.

A PRAYER TO CULTIVATE UNSHAKABLE FAITH

Heavenly Father,

I come before You today with a humble heart, acknowledging that all faith comes from You. I seek Your wisdom and strength to nurture and cultivate a faith that is firm and unwavering, regardless of the circumstances I may face. I understand that faith is not a one-time decision but a continual journey, and I ask for Your help to make it unshakable in my life. Lord, I desire to live a life that honors You and reflects Your greatness, knowing that this is only possible by grounding myself in Your promises and trusting in Your Word.

Your Scripture reminds me in **Romans 10:17 NKJV,** *"So then faith comes by hearing, and hearing by the word of God."* Father, I pray that I would immerse myself in Your Word each day, allowing Your truth to penetrate my heart and shape my mind. May Your Word be a light to guide my steps and a lamp to illuminate my path (Psalm 119:105), helping me navigate the challenges of life and teaching me to trust in Your will, even when the way forward is unclear.

In **Hebrews 11:1 NKJV**, we are reminded *"Now faith is the substance of things hoped for, the evidence of things not seen."* Lord, I ask that You strengthen my confidence in Your promises, even when I cannot yet see the outcome. Help me to trust in Your perfect timing and to stand firm on Your Word. When doubt arises, remind me of Your faithfulness in the past, for Your character remains constant, and You are always true to Your word.

In **James 1:5 NKJV,** You promise to give wisdom generously to all who ask. I ask You, Lord, to grant me the wisdom to deepen my faith. Open my eyes to the truths of Scripture, and help me understand how to apply Your Word in my daily life. May I seek You in prayer, and may Your wisdom guide my decisions so that I may live in a way that honors You and reflects Your will.

Father, You tell us in **Matthew 17:20 NKJV** that *"So Jesus said to them, 'Because of your unbelief; for assuredly, I say to you, if you have faith as a mustard seed, you will say to this mountain, "Move from here to there," and it will move; and nothing will be impossible for you."* I know, Lord, that even the smallest amount of faith, when placed in You, has the power to overcome immense challenges. Strengthen my faith so that no obstacle will seem insurmountable. Help me to believe that with You, nothing is impossible.

May I step forward in boldness, knowing that You are with me in every situation.

In **Mark 9:24 NKJV,** a father asks *"Immediately the father of the child cried out and said with tears, 'Lord, I believe; help my unbelief!"* Lord, I echo this prayer in my own life. There are moments when my faith falters and doubt creeps in. Strengthen me in these times of weakness and remind me of Your promises that never fail. Help me to walk by faith and not by sight (2 Corinthians 5:7), trusting that You are working all things for my good.

Philippians 4:6-7 NKJV encourages me to bring my concerns to You in prayer and petition, with thanksgiving. I pray that I would surrender all my anxieties to You, trusting in Your peace, which surpasses all understanding, to guard my heart and mind. As I cultivate unshakable faith, help me to rely on Your peace, knowing that You are always in control, no matter the circumstances.

In **Isaiah 40:31 NKJV,** You promise *"But those who wait on the Lord shall renew their strength; they shall mount up with wings like eagles, they shall run and not be weary, they shall walk and not faint."* Lord, I pray that as I place my hope in You, You will renew my strength and give me the endurance to keep going. May I keep my focus on You, the author and perfecter of my faith **Hebrews 12:2 NKJV,** knowing that You will empower me to persevere in the face of all challenges.

Lord, I also ask for the gift of perseverance, as taught in **Romans 5:3-4 NKJV**: *"And not only that, but we also glory in tribulations, knowing that tribulation produces perseverance; and perseverance, character; and character, hope."* Help me to see every trial as an opportunity for growth in faith and character. Teach me to persevere, trusting that You are refining me through every difficulty. May my life reflect Your faithfulness and serve as a testimony of Your love and power.

Thank You, Father, for the gift of faith. I surrender my heart to You and ask that You help me cultivate a faith that is unshakable and steadfast, regardless of the seasons of life. May I remain strong in my trust in You, knowing that You are always with me, guiding me, and strengthening me with every step I take.

In Jesus' name, I pray. ***Amen.***

CHAPTER NINE
LEAVING A LEGACY OF FAITH

A legacy is the lasting impression we make on other people's lives, not just the material belongings we amass or the ephemeral experiences we make. The most significant legacy for followers of Christ is not determined by material prosperity or honors, but rather by the faith we cultivate and transmit to next generations. Every choice we make, every action that reflects our faith, and every value we uphold becomes a seed planted in the hearts of those who come after us. Like the deep roots of a tree that enrich the soil for new life, a life firmly rooted in faith becomes a source of spiritual nourishment for everyone within its reach.

In this chapter, we examine the fundamental significance of leaving a legacy of unshakable faith—a legacy that is characterized by the sincere, dependable example of a life firmly anchored in trust in God, despite difficulties, rather than by perfection or material accomplishments. Together, we'll look at how to consciously leave this legacy, teach our kids religious principles, and make a profound, enduring difference in our communities and beyond.

Leaving a legacy of faith requires both wisdom and deliberate action. It is about embodying the love, hope, and peace that flow from a genuine relationship with Jesus Christ, allowing these virtues to guide every aspect of our lives. This legacy is built on the foundation of daily choices—choices that honor God and influence the people around us, whether they are family, friends, or even those we encounter briefly.

A legacy of faith transcends the confines of our own life and endures forever. It influences the present, makes a lasting impression on everyone we encounter, and motivates future generations. We may ensure that the influence of our lives lasts long after we are gone by planting seeds of faith that will develop and bloom as a result of living a life that reflects God's goodness and grace.

To build this legacy, we will turn to biblical examples, personal stories, and practical steps. Through these insights, we will discover how to live in a way that not only strengthens our own faith but also leaves an indelible mark on the hearts and lives of others—one that resonates into eternity. This chapter is designed to inspire and equip you to live in such a way that your faith becomes a powerful legacy, pointing others to Christ and creating a ripple effect that endures far beyond our earthly lives.

HOW TO PASS ON YOUR FAITH TO FUTURE GENERATIONS

Passing on a legacy of faith to future generations is not a task that occurs by chance; rather, it is a responsibility that demands intentionality, effort, and consistency. For parents, grandparents, mentors, and all those who seek to influence others, the foundation of this legacy begins in the home and extends outward into the community. Cultivating an unwavering faith in Jesus Christ requires more than just verbal instruction; it requires modeling a Christ-centered life that reflects the transformative power of the gospel. The way we live our lives—the choices we make, the way we handle adversity, and the love we extend to others—serves as a living testimony of our faith. Our actions speak volumes, and when they are aligned with God's Word, they serve as powerful examples for the next generation.

Equally important is the deliberate and consistent teaching of Scripture. The Bible is the foundation upon which our faith is built, and it is through immersing ourselves in God's Word that we gain wisdom, discernment, and a deeper understanding of His will. In **Deuteronomy 6:6-7 NKJV,** God instructs us to teach His commands to our children, talking about them *"And these words which I command you today shall be in your heart. You shall teach them diligently to your children, and shall talk of them when you sit in your house, when you walk by the way, when you lie down, and when you rise up."* This verse highlights the importance of integrating faith into every aspect of daily life, making it a constant presence in both our words and actions. By engaging in regular Bible study, prayer, and discussions about God's principles, we lay a foundation that helps children and others understand who God is and how they are to live in response to His love.

It is essential to establish an atmosphere in which faith is both actively experienced and taught. While knowing the Bible is important, people's hearts are changed when they experience God's presence firsthand.

This means sharing personal stories of God's faithfulness, encouraging people to seek God out when they are in need, and creating spaces where people may experience the peace and pleasure that come from living a life that is surrendered to Christ. The best way to spread faith is to demonstrate it through acts of service, love, and sacrifice in addition to verbal expression. When the next generation witnesses a genuine, lived-out faith, they are more likely to embrace it as their own, carrying the torch of faith forward to continue the legacy for years to come.

TEACH THROUGH WORDS AND ACTIONS

The way we teach, and model faith is of paramount importance when it comes to passing it on to future generations. It is not enough to merely speak words of wisdom and truth; we must ensure that our actions mirror those words, for it is through this alignment that our faith becomes both authentic and impactful.

As individuals who seek to inspire others, especially our children, students, or anyone under our influence, our lives must become a living testimony of the faith we profess. Our words must resonate with the same sincerity and commitment demonstrated through our actions, because only then can we truly impart the depth and power of God's message. The concept of this alignment between speech and deed is emphasized in the Bible, where we are called to embody the very teachings, we share.

In **Deuteronomy 6:6-7 NKJV,** the Bible instructs us to keep God's commandments close to our hearts and to impress them upon the hearts of our children. The verse specifically states, *"And these words which I command you today shall be in your heart. You shall teach them diligently to your children, and shall talk of them when you sit in your house, when you walk by the way, when you lie down, and when you rise up."*

Teaching and practicing one's faith should become a part of our everyday life rather than being limited to church services, Bible studies, or planned lessons, as this verse makes clear. According to this scripture, faith flourishes in the seemingly unremarkable times when we have the chance to show others God's compassion, mercy, and grace. The cornerstone of a faith that is both lived and taught is formed by deeds like praying together before meals, telling Bible stories together before bed, or being good to a neighbor.

Furthermore, the act of teaching faith through both words and actions fosters an environment of trust and consistency. When those around us, particularly children, observe that our actions reflect the values and teachings we espouse, they are more likely to internalize those values themselves. It is through this consistency that our faith becomes credible and tangible, for it is not simply a set of religious principles but a way of life that can be observed, experienced, and emulated.

In every interaction, we could reflect Christ-like values such as love, patience, humility, and forgiveness. By doing so, we show others that faith is not an abstract concept but a living force that shapes and transforms every aspect of our lives. Through our actions, we teach the next generation that faith is not something to be passively inherited but a vital, active part of who we are and how we relate to the world around us.

Spreading the faith requires more than just teaching people; it also means creating an atmosphere in which words and actions coexist. When we talk about God's kindness and then live in accordance with His Word, we not only teach others but also invite them to experience the transformative power of faith. By combining teaching with living, a legacy of faith is created that can be passed down to future generations, enabling them to follow in God's footsteps with assurance, hope, and steadfast faith.

MODELING A LIFE OF FAITH

The adage *"actions speak louder than words"* is frequently used, and it is especially relevant when discussing faith. Scripture, instruction, and words of encouragement are all unquestionably important, but our deeds are what ultimately have the biggest influence on others around us, particularly on young people and those who are easily influenced. It is our duty as leaders, mentors, and grownups to consciously live out the faith we claim to believe in because our actions speak louder than any sermon or instruction ever could.

This modeling involves living out the core of Christ's teachings in our everyday lives rather than just following a set of ceremonial rules. Paul encourages his audience to *"Imitate me, just as I also imitate Christ."* in **1 Corinthians 11:1 NKJV**. This invitation emphasizes how important setting a good example is for spiritual development and discipleship. We make the teachings of Christ concrete and approachable for others around us by setting an example.

When we speak of modeling a life of faith, we are referring not only to our outward actions but also to the attitudes, values, and principles that guide our decisions and interactions. Christ's life was characterized by love, compassion, forgiveness, humility, and unwavering trust in God's plan. As we strive to reflect these attributes, we provide others with a living example of how faith can transform our relationships, choices, and priorities.

Our ability to model Christ-like behavior becomes especially vital in times of adversity or struggle. In moments of difficulty, when the circumstances may be less than ideal, how we respond to challenges speaks volumes about the strength and authenticity of our faith.

Do we display patience and trust in God's sovereignty, or do we succumb to despair and frustration? Do we extend grace to those who wrong us, or do we harbor bitterness and resentment? It is through these responses, in both our everyday actions and our reactions to trials, that we teach others what it truly means to follow Jesus.

Furthermore, the example we set provides a foundation for future generations to build upon. Children and younger individuals learn much from watching the lives of those they respect and look up to. By living out our faith with integrity and consistency, we create a legacy that shapes their understanding of what it means to live a Christ-centered life.

This legacy is far more enduring than any doctrinal lesson we might impart, for it is through lived experience that faith becomes not merely an intellectual exercise but a way of life. When we model faith in our homes, workplaces, communities, and beyond, we instill in others the belief that faith is not a compartmentalized part of life but the very lens through which we view and navigate the world. This holistic approach to faith—where belief, actions, and values are intertwined—creates a powerful and compelling witness that others cannot ignore.

Providing a real-world example of what it means to follow Christ is the goal of modeling a life of faith. It's more about consistency, humility, and a readiness to put your faith in God's direction than it is about perfection. We provide others with the best example of the transformational power of faith by exhibiting the love, grace, patience, and hope of Christ.

By this, we are leaving a legacy that shall lead and encourage the relationship of God and the future generations. In the light of faith, we portray something more than conceptual or belief notions; it's a way of living which crafts our being and the way of livelihood.

THE ROLE OF FAITH IN SHAPING FAMILY AND COMMUNITY

Faith is more than just a personal path; it is a strong, transforming force that may influence not just the lives of individuals but also the fundamental structure of families and societies. When a family's foundation is faith, it provides a foundation for the growth of strong ties, the fostering of unity, and the encouragement of family members to better understand God's love and purpose for their life.

The influence of faith within the family unit is profound, as it shapes the values, actions, and priorities of each individual, creating an environment where love, support, and spiritual growth are central. Families grounded in faith are marked by a shared sense of purpose and mutual respect, where each person's unique talents and perspectives are valued, and their individual journeys are nurtured in the context of a larger, divinely-ordained plan.

The importance of faith within families extends beyond individual development; it also plays a critical role in fostering unity. A family that seeks to live out its faith in practical ways—through prayer, worship, service, and mutual encouragement—creates an environment where members can experience the unifying power of God's presence.

This unity is not merely about harmony or agreement, but about being united in a common purpose and a shared commitment to Christ. In **1 Corinthians 12:27 NKJV**, Paul describes the church as the *"body of Christ,"* emphasizing the importance of unity and shared purpose.

Just as the body functions most effectively when all its parts work together in harmony, a family or community that is centered on faith functions best when its members are united in their devotion to God and in their love for one another. Each individual, though unique in their strengths and weaknesses, contributes to the health and vitality of the whole, and it is through their collective commitment to God that they are able to thrive as a family.

Beyond the boundaries of the family, faith impacts the larger community. A community based on a common faith becomes a ray of hope, support, and change, much like a family founded on faith is an example of love and harmony. A community based on God's truth fosters an environment where people feel empowered to practice their religion and cooperate for the benefit of all.

In such a community, people are not defined by their differences but are bound together by the commonality of their shared beliefs and their commitment to serving others. The church, for instance, is a living example of how faith can unite people of diverse backgrounds, cultures, and experiences into a cohesive body with a single mission: to spread God's love and truth to the world.

Moreover, faith has the ability to transform not just relationships within families and communities, but the very culture in which they exist. A society that values faith in God is one that upholds principles of justice, mercy, and compassion.

The impact of a faith-centered family and community extends outward, influencing broader societal norms and encouraging a culture that prioritizes care for the marginalized, justice for the oppressed, and peace in the midst of conflict. When individuals come together with a shared commitment to live out their faith, they become agents of change, working to bring about God's kingdom here on earth.

Faith is an important building block within families and society. It provides the base for the relationships, it's the cement holding them together, and the agent of change in equipping people to live out God's love practically day in and day out. This paper helps a person build an atmosphere within the family, church, and the larger community better prepared to seek the mind and the purpose of God. Such a family or community, as far as the commitment to Christ goes, becomes an example of his love, grace, and unity that one can live. A window of transformation brought in by faith and representative of the God Kingdom here on earth.

FAITH IN THE FAMILY

A family rooted in faith provides the essential foundation for love, respect, and grace to not only survive but flourish. This solid spiritual groundwork creates a safe and nurturing environment in which each member can experience and express unconditional love, develop a deep sense of self-worth, and cultivate meaningful relationships based on mutual respect and understanding.

In **Joshua 24:15 NKJV,** the steadfast leader Joshua makes a bold declaration: *"And if it seems evil to you to serve the Lord, choose for yourselves this day whom you will serve, whether the gods which your fathers served that were on the other side of the river, or the gods of the Amorites, in whose land you dwell. But as for me and my house, we will serve the Lord."* This powerful statement highlights the profound truth that faith is not simply an individual pursuit but a collective decision that shapes the very fabric of the family. By intentionally choosing to serve God together, families reinforce their commitment to one another and to the divine purpose that unites them.

When a family makes the decision to walk in faith together, the effects extend far beyond just their personal relationship with God. Their commitment to God's will fosters a deeper sense of unity, trust, and cohesion among family members.

By placing God at the center of their lives, family members learn to navigate challenges with grace, offer forgiveness with a pure heart, and extend patience in times of frustration. These virtues, deeply rooted in faith, form the backbone of a strong and loving family dynamic.

As parents, grandparents, or guardians model faith-based values, children absorb these principles, creating a cycle of spiritual growth and moral development that is passed down through generations. The faith that is nurtured within the family unit becomes a legacy, ensuring that each successive generation will carry the torch of faith into the future with a sense of purpose, responsibility, and unwavering devotion to God.

Moreover, a family built on faith serves as a powerful witness to the larger community, demonstrating how love and respect can thrive when rooted in a shared belief in God. The way a family interacts with one another—showing grace in difficult times, offering support when one is struggling, and prioritizing reconciliation over division—becomes an example of Christ's love for the world. It is in the everyday moments of family life that faith is most vividly expressed, through simple acts of kindness, shared prayers, and moments of reflection that reaffirm God's presence in their lives.

These practices not only strengthen the family's internal bonds but also create a ripple effect, influencing the wider community and inspiring others to build their relationships on a foundation of faith.

As such, a family that serves the Lord together fosters a spiritual legacy that impacts not only its own members but the broader community as well. By prioritizing faith in their daily lives, families provide a secure and loving environment for all to grow spiritually, emotionally, and relationally. In doing so, they prepare the next generation to carry on the torch of faith, equipping them with the moral compass and spiritual foundation needed to navigate life's challenges and to serve as beacons of hope and love in a world that desperately needs it. Through this intentional, God-centered approach to family life, a legacy of faith is not merely spoken—it is lived, and it has the power to transform not only individual lives but entire communities.

FAITH BEYOND THE FAMILY: SHAPING COMMUNITY

Faith is not meant to be confined within the walls of our homes—it extends far beyond, reaching into the broader community and transforming the world around us. When we actively live out our faith in our neighborhoods, workplaces, schools, and churches, we become agents of change, contributing to the building of a society that reflects the principles of God's Kingdom.

Jesus, in **Matthew 5:14 NKJV**, calls His followers to be the *"light of the world,"* emphasizing the vital role believers play in illuminating the darkness of the world with God's truth. Our actions in the public sphere—whether through acts of kindness, justice, compassion, or love—become a powerful witness to others, encouraging them to reflect on their own spiritual lives and, potentially, inspiring them to seek God for themselves.

Living out our faith publicly provides a tangible example of the transformative power of a life devoted to Christ. When others witness the fruits of faith—such as integrity in the workplace, selflessness in relationships, and a heart for service—it sparks curiosity about the source of this change. It opens the door for meaningful conversations about Christ and His love for humanity, creating opportunities to share the gospel and inspire others to consider the difference that faith can make in their own lives.

In this way, our actions become more than mere demonstrations of virtue; they become invitations to experience the peace, hope, and joy that come from a relationship with Jesus.

In addition to individual actions, faith in the community has a ripple effect that can lead to collective transformation. When believers come together to serve their communities—whether through outreach programs, charitable initiatives, or social justice efforts—they reflect the love and grace of God in tangible ways.

These acts of service, when rooted in faith, not only meet the immediate needs of others but also reveal the heart of God for the marginalized and oppressed. As believers work together to address societal issues, they embody Christ's call to love our neighbors as ourselves, creating a community that reflects God's values of justice, mercy, and compassion.

In conclusion, passing on a legacy of faith requires intentionality, consistency, and love. By teaching and modeling a life of faith through both words and actions, we lay the foundation for future generations to continue the work of advancing God's Kingdom. As we nurture relationships that reflect Christ's love, both within our families and beyond, we contribute to the building of a faith-filled community that will carry the light of God's truth into the world.

Through these efforts, we leave an unshakable imprint on the world, one that will endure for years to come, impacting lives and shaping the future for generations yet unborn. In this way, our faith becomes a powerful, transformative force not only in our homes but throughout society, continually reflecting God's glory and love.

BIBLE STORY: THE EARLY CHURCH'S IMPACT ON THE COMMUNITY

In **Acts 2:44-47 NKJV**, the early church is depicted as a community deeply rooted in faith and unity, where believers shared everything, they had and cared for one another's needs. The passage states, *"Now all who believed were together, and had all things in common, and sold their possessions and goods, and divided them among all, as anyone had need. So, continuing daily with one accord in the temple, and breaking bread from house to house, they ate their food with gladness and simplicity of heart, praising God and having favor with all the people. And the Lord added to the church daily those who were being saved."* This description of the early church highlights their commitment to living out their faith through practical acts of love, generosity, and unity.

They did not just speak of faith—they embodied it in every aspect of their lives. This vibrant and selfless community became a powerful witness of God's love, drawing others to Christ. The impact of their collective faith was profound, as their actions demonstrated the transformative power of living according to the teachings of Jesus. Their example of communal living left a lasting legacy, not only in their time but also in how the church continues to impact communities today.

ENCOURAGING OTHERS TO STAND STRONG IN FAITH

As we build a lasting legacy of faith, one of the most vital responsibilities we have is to encourage others—especially the next generation—to stand firm in their faith. In the face of the world's challenges and adversities, it can often feel as though hope is fleeting, and the pressures of life threaten to shake our resolve.

Indeed, the trials and difficulties that we encounter in our personal lives and in society at large can sometimes feel overwhelming, and at times, they may tempt us to question God's goodness or to become disheartened. In these moments of uncertainty and hardship, it is essential for us, as members of the body of Christ, to lift one another up, to speak words of encouragement, and to remind each other of the unshakable truths of God's promises.

The Scripture consistently exhorts us to encourage one another in the faith. **Hebrews 10:24-25 NKJV** urges us to *""And let us consider one another in order to stir up love and good works, not forsaking the assembling of ourselves together, as is the manner of some, but exhorting one another, and so much the more as you see the Day approaching."* This emphasizes the value of community in maintaining our faith since it allows us to continue in our relationship with God via camaraderie and support from one another. We are expected to walk together, to bear each other's burdens, and to support one another in maintaining our faith in Christ. We are not supposed to face life's challenges alone.

Furthermore, it is crucial that we, especially as mentors to the next generation, model a faith that is resilient and unwavering, demonstrating that God's promises are reliable and trustworthy even in the most trying of circumstances. Just as the Apostle Paul exhorted Timothy to *"fan into flame the gift of God"* that was in him, we too must fan into flame the faith of those who are entrusted to our care.

By offering support, guidance, and words of wisdom, we can help others to build their own firm foundation in faith. This is particularly important for young people, who may be navigating a world filled with confusion and uncertainty. We must teach them that faith is not merely a passive belief, but an active, living force that has the power to transform lives and sustain them through life's storms.

In addition to offering verbal encouragement, we can also demonstrate steadfast faith through our actions. When we live with conviction and confidence in God's promises, we provide others with a living testimony of His faithfulness. Our actions speak louder than words, and as we model resilience in the face of adversity, we inspire others to do the same.

The Apostle James reminds us that *"knowing that the testing of your faith produces patience."* **James 1:3 NKJV**, and by sharing our own stories of perseverance and triumph, we encourage others to trust in God's ability to see them through their own trials. It is through these shared experiences of faith that we create a community of believers who are strengthened by one another and empowered to stand strong in the face of challenges.

As we work to pass on a legacy of faith, one of the most powerful tools we have is the encouragement we offer to others. By uplifting those around us, reminding them of God's promises, and modeling a life of resilient faith, we help to create a culture of trust and perseverance that spans generations. Whether through words, actions, or shared experiences, we play an integral role in supporting others as they grow in their own faith. In doing so, we contribute to the building of a strong, united body of believers who can stand firm in their trust in God, no matter what obstacles or trials they may face.

IMPORTANCE OF BEING A FAITHFUL EXAMPLE

Our actions and lives serve as a profound and compelling witness to the faith we profess. The example we set for others is often one of the most powerful ways we can encourage and strengthen those around us in their spiritual journey. Just as our own faith has been shaped by the faithful examples of those who have gone before us, we have a God-given responsibility to become living examples of faith for others, especially for those who are younger in their walk with God or newer to the Christian faith.

In **1 Peter 5:3 NKJV,** the apostle Peter urges leaders within the church to be *"examples to the flock,"* emphasizing that this principle is not limited to church leaders but is applicable to all believers. As followers of Christ, we are called to reflect His love, His character, and His faithfulness in every area of our lives, whether within the confines of our families, our workplaces, or our broader communities. When we live out our faith with consistency and authenticity, we become living testimonies of God's goodness and His transformative power.

Living out a faithful example does not merely involve preaching the gospel through words but primarily through actions. In our daily lives, we have the opportunity to embody the principles of love, patience, kindness, and perseverance, particularly in the face of hardship. The manner in which we handle difficult situations, navigate challenges, and respond to adversity speaks volumes about the depth of our faith.

Our joy in the midst of trials, our perseverance in times of suffering, and our unwavering hope in the promises of God all serve as powerful models to others. When others see our steadfast faith in God's provision and goodness, even during difficult circumstances, they are encouraged to hold fast to their own trust in God. Our example provides a tangible and relatable model for others to follow—one that demonstrates that faith is not merely theoretical but a living, active force that sustains us through life's trials.

In fact, our example has the potential to inspire others to develop a deeper trust in God's faithfulness, even when the road ahead seems uncertain.

Just as the apostle Paul encouraged the church in **1 Corinthians 11:1 NKJV** *to "Imitate me, just as I also imitate Christ."* we, too, can inspire others to live in accordance with God's will by modeling Christlike behavior in our own lives.

The strength of our example becomes particularly significant in the context of community. When those around us observe our consistent commitment to our faith, especially when faced with adversity, it strengthens the collective resolve of the community. The ability to witness God's faithfulness in one person's life serves as a reminder to others that God is equally present and faithful in their own circumstances. This becomes a cycle of encouragement, where one person's testimony strengthens the faith of another, creating a dynamic and supportive environment for spiritual growth.

Furthermore, the consistency with which we live out our faith has long-lasting implications. Our example can shape the faith of future generations. For parents, mentors, and leaders, the way we choose to live our lives has the potential to influence those who come after us, teaching them how to walk in faith through both the blessings and the challenges of life.

A faithful example can inspire those who are younger or less experienced in the faith to rise above the doubts and distractions of the world and to remain steadfast in their trust in God. As we model godliness, integrity, and love, we provide a foundation for others to build their faith upon, encouraging them to stand firm in their own relationship with Christ.

The early church's impact on its surrounding community serves as a timeless example of how the faithful example of believers can draw others to Christ. The unity, love, and faithfulness demonstrated by the early Christians were powerful testimonies that led many to faith in Jesus Christ.

As we build a legacy of faith, we are called to encourage and strengthen one another, especially during times of trial and difficulty. By being faithful examples of God's love, grace, and endurance, we can inspire others to stand firm in their faith, trusting that God will use both our trials and our victories to strengthen and shape the faith of future generations. The power of a faithful example is immeasurable—it has the potential to inspire, uplift, and lead others to experience the transforming power of a life devoted to Christ.

A PERSONAL TESTIMONY OF LEAVING A LEGACY OF UNSHAKABLE FAITH

The journey of my life has been a mosaic of trials and triumphs, each thread—woven with moments of pain, perseverance, and victory—shaping the foundation of my faith. Through every challenge and each moment of joy, I have been sustained by the hand of God, a hand that has never wavered, never let me go, even in the darkest of times.

As I reflect on my life's story, it is not merely a personal narrative but one that has intertwined with the lives of my children, my family, and my friends. They have walked beside me, not just as witnesses to my struggles and successes, but as living testimonies of God's unfailing love and faithfulness. And as I share these experiences with them, I hope to ignite the same unshakable faith in their hearts, so they, too, can trust in the steadfastness of God's promises.

There is one truth I hold dear, one truth that I have repeated time and time again to my children: *"I cannot live without God, without Jesus Christ in my life."* This declaration is not just a phrase—it is the very breath of my existence, the pulse that beats in my chest, and the anchor that has kept me from sinking into despair. It is the cornerstone of my faith, the foundation of my journey.

I have seen time and again that in the fiercest storms of life, God is my refuge, and in the stillness of His presence, I find peace. ***Psalms 62:5-6 NKJV*** affirms this truth: *"My soul, wait silently for God alone, For my expectation is from Him. He only is my rock and my salvation; He is my defense; I shall not be moved."* Through my words, actions, and decisions, I seek to embody this trust in God, making His faithfulness visible to my children and all those who walk beside me.

However, this legacy of faith is not confined solely to my family. The people in my everyday life—my friends, co-workers, neighbors, and even strangers—have also seen the undeniable hand of God at work. They observe the peace that surpasses understanding, the joy that remains when circumstances are bleak, and the grace that flows through me in moments of difficulty.

As Jesus encourages in **Matthew 5:16 NKJV,** *"Let your light so shine before men, that they may see your good works and glorify your Father in heaven."* I have the firm belief that it is not only within me for my good but that this light in Christ can further become a guiding beacon to show others to this most powerful and strong love of God that transforms everything and redeems. My life is not mine; it's a testament to His greatness, a reflection of His glory.

My deepest prayer is that my children—and all who observe my life—will be moved to cultivate their own unshakable faith, a faith rooted in the undeniable evidence of God's presence and power. **Psalms 145:4 NKJV** speaks directly to this calling: *"One generation shall praise Your works to another, And shall declare Your mighty acts."* This verse reverberates within me, reminding me of the sacred responsibility to pass on a legacy of faith that magnifies God's glory. In every trial, in every triumph, I pray that my steadfast trust in God will be a testament to His faithfulness, serving as an example for my children and others to follow.

The trials I have faced, the struggles I have endured, and the victories I have achieved have not been for my own personal growth alone. They are seeds planted in the hearts of those around me, seeds that, by God's grace, will grow into a harvest of faith. As **Romans 8:28 NKJV** reminds us, *"And we know that all things work together for good to those who love God, to those who are the called according to His purpose."* Even when the path seemed unclear or the road seemed impossible, God was at work. My life has become a living proclamation of His truth—evidencing that His promises never fail, that His love is unchanging, and that He is always near.

Through the power of God's grace, I have been able to stand firm in the face of adversity, not because of my own strength, but because of His. In each trial, I have been carried by His love, and in each victory, I have been reminded that it is He who empowers me to overcome. And as I pass this legacy of faith on to my children, I trust that it will ripple through their lives and the lives of others, inspiring them to trust in God's faithfulness and to build their own unshakable faith in Him.

It is my deepest desire that this legacy will continue to unfold long after I am gone. My hope is that, through the life I've lived, others will see a life surrendered to Christ—a life marked by hope, courage, and unwavering trust in God's promises. And as they encounter the light of Christ in me, they, too, will be drawn to His love and grace. As **2 Corinthians 5: NKJV** says, *"For we live by faith, not by sight."* And so, I will continue to live, not by what I can see with my eyes, but by the faith that God has planted in my heart—faith that has been tested, refined, and proven true through every trial, and faith that will endure for generations to come.

May my life, with all its imperfections and triumphs, serve as a reminder that God is faithful to all who trust in Him, and that His love and power will sustain us, now and forever.

Conclusion

Leaving a legacy of unshakable faith is not defined solely by what we do but by the essence of who we are—individuals who trust wholeheartedly in God's promises and strive to align our lives with His truth. It is through teaching our faith, living it authentically, and encouraging others to embrace it that we have the privilege of shaping a legacy that extends far beyond our lifetime. This legacy of faith is not confined to words or occasional deeds but is embedded in the daily choices we make, the values we uphold, and the relationships we nurture within our families and communities. When we live intentionally, prioritizing faith in every aspect of life, we contribute to a narrative that points others to Jesus Christ and His transformative love.

The most enduring legacy we can leave behind is a life that bears witness to the power and steadfastness of faith in Jesus Christ. This legacy is not about perfection but about persistence—walking in trust even in the face of challenges, demonstrating love in moments of difficulty, and clinging to hope when the road ahead seems uncertain. When others see the light of Christ reflected in our lives, they are inspired to seek Him for themselves and to build their own legacy of faith. It is through our example that future generations can come to know the depth of God's love and the strength of His promises.

Like Timothy's grandmother Lois and his mother Eunice, who are remembered in Scripture for their faithful influence, we are called to be intentional in passing down a legacy that endures. Their example reminds us of the power of faith passed from one generation to the next, creating a ripple effect that glorifies God and impacts countless lives. By faithfully living out our beliefs and investing in those around us, we ensure that the seeds of faith we plant today will grow into a flourishing testament to God's glory for generations to come.

Ultimately, the legacy of unshakable faith is not measured by earthly accolades but by the spiritual fruit it bears in the lives of others. It is a legacy that transcends time, echoing into eternity as lives are transformed by the love and grace of Jesus Christ. May we each be steadfast in our commitment to live a life that reflects God's goodness and inspires others to follow Him. In doing so, we fulfill our calling to be faithful stewards of the faith entrusted to us, leaving a profound and enduring impact that brings glory to God for generations yet unborn.

A PRAYER FOR LEAVING A LEGACY OF FAITH

Heavenly Father,

I come before You with a heart full of gratitude and reverence for the unwavering faithfulness You have shown in my life. Lord, I recognize that the greatest gift I can leave behind is a legacy rooted in an unshakable faith in You. It is my deepest desire to leave a mark on my family, my community, and all who come after me—a mark that points them to the hope, peace, and love found only in You.

Your Word, Father, reminds us in **Deuteronomy 6:6-7 NKJV**, *"And these words which I command you today shall be in your heart. You shall teach them diligently to your children, and shall talk of them when you sit in your house, when you walk by the way, when you lie down, and when you rise up."* I ask for Your help in being intentional in teaching the next generation about Your goodness, Your faithfulness, and Your boundless love. May my life reflect Your truth, and may my words and actions spark a desire in my children and those around me to seek You. Let them see Your love in the way I live and be drawn closer to You.

Lord, in **Psalms 78:4 NKJV**, You call us to *"We will not hide them from their children, telling to the generation to come the praises of the Lord, and His strength and His wonderful works that He has done."* I pray that I would be faithful in sharing the testimony of Your work in my life. Help me to recount the stories of Your provision, healing, and guidance, so that those who come after me may place their full trust in You. May my life be a living testament to Your greatness, and may my faithfulness inspire others to walk in Your truth.

Father, I also ask that You help me live in such a way that others are drawn to the faith I hold in You. As **Matthew 5:14-16 NKJV** declares, *"You are the light of the world. A city that is set on a hill cannot be hidden. Nor do they light a lamp and put it under a basket, but on a lampstand, and it gives light to all who are in the house. Let your light so shine before men, that they* *may see your good works and glorify your Father in heaven."* Lord, let my life reflect Your light, shining brightly for others to see. May my actions speak louder than my words and point others toward You.

In **Proverbs 22:6 NKJV,** You instruct us to *"Train up a child in the way he should go, And when he is old he will not depart from it."* Father, I trust You with the hearts of my children and the children of future generations. As I invest in their spiritual growth, guide them in Your ways. May the seeds of faith I plant today take root in their hearts and grow into a strong, unshakable faith that endures for generations to come.

Lord, I also acknowledge that a legacy of faith is built not only through words, but through actions. In **1 Corinthians 11:1 NKJV**, Paul urges us *"Imitate me, just as I also imitate Christ."* I pray that my life would be one that others can follow, as I strive to imitate Christ in every aspect. Let my faith be visible in my daily choices—in how I love, forgive, and serve others. May I reflect Your character, so that others may see You in me.

Father, my greatest desire is to leave behind a legacy that glorifies You. May my children, my family, and all who come after me be able to say they have witnessed Your goodness and love through my life. Let the legacy I leave be one that points others to You and brings honor to Your name.

In **2 Timothy 1:5 NKJV,** Paul commended the faith of Timothy's mother and grandmother, saying, *"When I call to remembrance the genuine faith that is in you, which dwelt first in your grandmother Lois and your mother*

Eunice, and I am persuaded is in you also." I pray that my faith, like theirs, would be passed down from generation to generation. May my children and grandchildren walk in the faith I have modeled and experience the same depth of relationship with You that I have known.

Father, thank You for the opportunity to build a legacy of faith. Help me remain faithful in this sacred task, and may my life honor You in everything I do. May the legacy I leave be one of steadfast trust in You, a legacy that points others to the hope of eternal life found in Jesus Christ.

In Jesus' name, I pray.

Amen.

CONCLUSION

As we arrive at the conclusion of this exploration of unshakable faith, we are reminded of an enduring truth: faith in Jesus Christ is neither transient nor abstract. It is a dynamic, living force that has the capacity to transform lives, overcome insurmountable obstacles, and anchor us through the most turbulent storms of life.

True faith is not passive; it is active, steadfast, and relentless. It empowers us to stand firm when the ground beneath us feels unsteady and when the uncertainties of life threaten to overwhelm us.

Throughout this journey, we have delved into the transformative power of unshakable faith—a faith that equips us to face trials with courage, trust in God's plan even when it seems unclear, and build a legacy that extends far beyond our time on this earth. Faith is not merely a concept to be pondered; it is the solid foundation upon which lives rich in purpose, peace, and hope are constructed. Through faith, we gain access to God's immeasurable strength, experience His comforting presence, and become instruments of His love and truth in a world desperately in need of both.

To stand firm in faith is to embrace an active posture rooted in the unchanging character of God. It means choosing to trust in His promises and relying not on our limited strength but on His infinite power. The foundation of our stability lies in His faithfulness, and His Word serves as the anchor that keeps us steady in the face of life's tempests. Faith is not confined to verbal declarations; it is demonstrated through our actions, reflected in our decisions, and evident in our relationships.

In moments of trial, when doubt and fear threaten to take hold, standing firm in faith becomes all the more crucial. These are the times when faith allows us to see beyond our immediate struggles and discern God's providential hand at work. It gives us the assurance that He is orchestrating all things for our good, even when the outcome remains unseen. Faith equips us with the resilience to endure, trusting that God's plans for us are not only good but also perfectly timed.

The cultivation of unshakable faith is a lifelong endeavor. Just as a tree develops deep roots to weather storms, our faith must be firmly grounded in the truth of Scripture and nurtured through prayer, worship, and reflection on God's past faithfulness. This intentional growth ensures that our faith remains strong and unwavering, enabling us to navigate life's challenges with confidence and peace.

Equally significant is our role in encouraging others to stand firm in their faith. Faith is not a solitary pursuit but a shared journey. By offering support, sharing our testimonies, and interceding for one another in prayer, we contribute to the strength and unity of the body of Christ. Our stories of God's faithfulness serve as beacons of hope, inspiring others to trust Him even in the most trying circumstances.

As we reflect on the insights and truths explored in this book, it becomes evident that unshakable faith is more than a theological ideal—it is a daily commitment. It is a deliberate choice to trust God, to rely on His promises, and to live in the light of His truth, regardless of the challenges we face. Faith shapes our character, enriches our relationships, and influences the world around us. It is the source of our courage, the wellspring of our hope, and the foundation of the legacy we leave behind.

We are invited to stand firm in our faith, to hold steadfastly to the promises of God, and to step forward with courage and conviction. The legacy of faith we create is the greatest gift we can offer, one that reflects the enduring power of Christ's love, truth, and grace. This legacy has the potential to inspire generations to come, drawing them closer to the heart of God and equipping them to live lives of purpose and hope.

As we move forward, may we do so with the unwavering assurance that God is faithful to complete the work He has begun in us. Let us stand firm in the power of faith, trusting in His perfect plan, and living lives that honor and glorify Him in all things. Unshakable faith is not only our refuge but also our greatest testimony, and it is through this faith that we can impact the world for Christ and leave an eternal imprint on the lives of others.

A FINAL WORD ON HOLDING FAST TO UNSHAKABLE FAITH

Faith, like any meaningful relationship, demands intentional investment and unwavering trust. It is easy to feel confident in our faith and trust in God when life is smooth and everything is going well. However, the true strength of unshakable faith is revealed not in times of peace but in moments of hardship and adversity.

It is in the midst of trials that our faith is truly tested, refined, and ultimately strengthened. **James 1:2-4 NKJV** offers us an important perspective on this process: *"My brethren, count it all joy when you fall into various trials, knowing that the testing of your faith produces patience. But let patience have its perfect work, that you may be perfect and complete, lacking nothing."*

These verses remind us that the difficulties we face in life are not indicators of God's absence or neglect, but rather they are opportunities for us to deepen our experience of His power and grace. When we face challenges, our faith is not only tested but refined, much like gold that is purified in fire. Just as a blacksmith uses heat to mold metal into something stronger and more valuable, God uses life's trials to shape and fortify our faith. Through these trials, we are molded into the image of Christ, growing in maturity, perseverance, and a deeper understanding of God's sovereignty over every circumstance.

It is important to recognize that trials and difficulties are not random or pointless. They are divinely appointed moments in our journey, carefully designed by God to build in us the character traits we need to become the people He has called us to be. Through these experiences, our faith is not only tested but also strengthened, just as physical muscles become stronger when put through resistance training. When we persevere through difficulties, we develop resilience that carries us through future trials and deepens our trust in God.

As we hold fast to God's Word and continue to trust in His faithfulness, we find assurance in passages such as **Philippians 1:6 NKJV,** which says, *"Being confident of this very thing, that He who has begun a good work in you will complete it until the day of Jesus Christ."* This promise is a source of immense comfort. It assures us that God is always at work within us, even when we cannot see the full picture. His work in our lives is not temporary or fleeting; it is a continuous process of transformation, shaping us into the people He desires us to be.

No matter the trials or obstacles we face, we can have complete confidence in the fact that God is faithful to His promises. He is committed to completing the good work He has begun in us, and He will never leave us or forsake us. His promises are firm and unwavering, and His love for us is constant. When life feels uncertain or overwhelming, we can hold tightly to the knowledge that God is not only with us in our struggles but that He is using these experiences to prepare us for the future and to accomplish His greater purpose in our lives.

Unshakable faith is built over time, nurtured through both triumphs and trials. It is strengthened as we choose to trust in God's goodness, even when the circumstances around us seem to suggest otherwise. The key to holding fast to our faith is not relying on our own strength or understanding, but on the strength and promises of God. When we lean into His Word, when we reflect on His faithfulness throughout our lives, and when we remember His enduring love, we find the courage and endurance to stand firm in faith, no matter what challenges come our way.

In the journey of faith, we must remind ourselves constantly that God is faithful, even in the moments of hardship. It is through adversity that we often come to know God in a deeper, more intimate way, experiencing His love, power, and faithfulness in ways we could never have imagined during times of ease. Our faith is not merely a passive belief—it is a living, breathing trust that grows stronger as we continue to lean on God and rely on His strength.

In the end, holding fast to unshakable faith means embracing God's promises with confidence, trusting that He is with us through every storm, and allowing Him to use our trials for our good and His glory. No matter what life throws our way, we can rest in the assurance that God is working all things together for our good and that, through our steadfast faith, we will be made complete in Christ.

Encouragement to Trust God Every Day

Faith is not a one-time decision or a fleeting emotion; it is a daily practice, a continual commitment to trust God in every moment. Every day presents us with unique challenges and opportunities, and our response to those challenges reveals the depth of our faith.

Trusting God doesn't happen only in the big, life-altering moments—it must be cultivated in the quiet moments, the mundane routines, and the struggles we face on a daily basis. The Bible reminds us in **Matthew 6:34 NKJV**, *"Therefore do not worry about tomorrow, for tomorrow will worry about its own things. Sufficient for the day is its own trouble."* This verse offers a profound insight into the nature of faith: while we may be tempted to worry about what lies ahead, we are called to focus on the present, trusting that God is with us in every moment.

Each new day presents us with its own set of challenges—things we didn't anticipate, obstacles we didn't foresee, and struggles that test our patience, resilience, and faith. Yet, in each of these moments, we also find fresh opportunities to trust God. While we cannot predict the future, we do know the One who holds the future.

Our faith allows us to let go of our anxieties about tomorrow and embrace the present, knowing that God's care for us extends to every part of our lives. When we trust in His sovereignty and His perfect plan, we can rest in the knowledge that He is guiding us through each day, no matter what challenges it brings.

In the midst of our uncertainties, we find peace in knowing that God's provision is sufficient for every moment. Even when we feel overwhelmed by the weight of the world, we can trust that He is our refuge and strength. **Isaiah 41:10 NKJV** offers us a powerful reminder of God's unwavering presence and support: *"Fear not, for I am with you; Be not dismayed, for I am your God. I will strengthen you, Yes, I will help you, I will uphold you with My righteous right hand."* This promise is not just a comforting thought; it is a declaration of God's faithfulness. When life seems too heavy to bear, we are assured that we are not alone in our struggles. God is with us, strengthening us, helping us, and holding us steady with His powerful right hand.

In the face of daily trials, we may be tempted to try and handle everything ourselves, relying on our own understanding, strength, and resources. But trusting God every day requires us to acknowledge that we cannot carry the burdens of life on our own. It is an invitation to surrender our fears, worries, and plans to Him, knowing that He will provide exactly what we need in each moment. This kind of trust involves letting go of control and embracing the truth that God's ways are higher than our own and that He is infinitely wiser and more capable than we are.

Moreover, trusting God every day is not just about asking Him for help when things get tough—it's also about recognizing His presence in the quiet moments, in the routine, and in the small blessings that we may overlook. It is in the mundane where God often works in the most subtle yet profound ways. Each new day is an opportunity to deepen our faith, to acknowledge His faithfulness, and to thank Him for His constant provision.

As we journey through life, the key to trusting God daily is consistency. It is choosing to set our eyes on Him each day, even when the future seems unclear or daunting. It is taking time to remind ourselves of His promises and to speak those truths over our lives. It is choosing to trust His plan even when we cannot see the full picture, knowing that He is working all things together for our good. Trusting God is not a one-time act of surrender but an ongoing decision to rely on Him in all circumstances, big and small.

When we choose to trust God every day, we allow His peace to guard our hearts and minds, even in the midst of uncertainty. **Philippians 4:6-7 NKJV** encourages us to bring our concerns before God in prayer, and in exchange, He offers us peace that surpasses all understanding. This peace does not come from knowing what tomorrow holds, but from knowing that God holds tomorrow. It is the peace that comes when we trust that He is in control, no matter the circumstances.

Ultimately, learning to trust God every day is an invitation to experience the fullness of His love, grace, and power. It is in daily moments of surrender that we grow in our relationship with Him, and it is through those moments that our faith becomes unshakable. By trusting God with the present and leaving the future in His hands, we can walk confidently through each day, knowing that He will never leave us or forsake us.

So, as you go about your day, remember that trust is not just a single decision—it is a daily choice. Each day offers a new opportunity to trust in God's wisdom, His provision, and His perfect plan for your life. And as you trust Him with the small and large moments alike, you will find that His presence is always with you, strengthening you, upholding you, and guiding you every step of the way.

Moving Forward with Courage and Unwavering Faith

As you journey forward in life, it is essential to not only reflect on the lessons you've learned but also to actively apply them. Unshakable faith is not merely a passive belief, but a dynamic force that drives us to act, to persevere, and to trust God in every circumstance. True faith is a call to action—it is about taking the truths we hold dear and allowing them to shape our decisions, behaviors, and attitudes.

The apostle Paul reminds us of this in **2 Corinthians 5:7 NKJV,** when he declares *"For we walk by faith, not by sight."* This verse encapsulates the core principle of living out our faith: even when we cannot see the full picture or understand how things will unfold, we continue to move forward with trust and courage. Our ability to keep going does not rely on our own understanding, but on the trust that God's plan for our lives is good and that He will guide us every step of the way.

Faith is not defined by certainty in the visible; it is the confident assurance in the unseen. This is a key characteristic of unshakable faith: the ability to trust in God's promises even when the circumstances seem to contradict them. **Hebrews 11:1 NKJV** provides a powerful definition of faith *"Now faith is the substance of things hoped for, the evidence of things not seen."* In other words, faith is the ability to hold onto the hope of what we cannot yet see, anchored in the firm belief that God's Word is true, and His promises are reliable.

This kind of faith goes beyond mere belief—it involves trusting that God's plan will unfold in His perfect timing, even when we don't understand the immediate path ahead.

As we move forward in faith, we must remember that the foundation of our courage is not based on our own abilities or strength. The power to stand firm in faith comes from the Holy Spirit, who resides within every believer. **Romans 8:1 NKJV** powerfully assures us, *"There is therefore now no condemnation to those who are in Christ Jesus, who do not walk according to the flesh, but according to the Spirit."*

The same power that raised Jesus from the dead is at work within us. This truth is a source of immeasurable strength—it means that, regardless of the challenges we face, we are empowered to persevere with courage. The Holy Spirit provides us with the inner strength to rise above our circumstances, to stand firm, and to keep moving forward even when the road ahead seems uncertain.

Courage does not come from the absence of fear but from the presence of faith. Unshakable faith enables us to move forward with confidence, even in the midst of uncertainty. We may not have all the answers, but we trust in the One who does. Courage in the Christian life is not about blind optimism; it is rooted in the assurance that God is with us, that He will never leave us nor forsake us **Deuteronomy 31:6 NKJV.** Our faith in Him becomes the anchor that keeps us steady amidst life's storms, and it compels us to step out in obedience, trusting that He will lead us every step of the way.

As we move forward, it's important to remember that unshakable faith is not a one-time decision, but a daily choice. It is a continual commitment to trust God, even when we don't understand the reasons behind the challenges we face. Our faith grows stronger when we choose to rely on God's promises, when we choose to step into the unknown with the confidence that He is in control. It's through these moments of active faith that we become vessels for God's glory, not only for our own benefit but for the sake of others who are watching our journey.

There will be times when we will face obstacles that seem insurmountable. There will be moments when we are tempted to doubt, to shrink back, or to give up altogether. Yet, it is in these moments that we must stand firm in what we know to be true: that God is faithful, that His Word is a firm foundation, and that His presence is with us every step of the way. Courage in the Christian life is not about being fearless; it is about choosing to press on in the face of fear, with the confidence that God is with us.

As we step forward with unwavering faith, let us also be mindful of the responsibility we have to share this faith with others. Our journey is not just for ourselves but for those around us. When others see our faith in action—when they witness our ability to stand firm in difficult circumstances—they are encouraged and inspired to trust God for themselves. Our courage in the face of adversity can serve as a beacon of hope to others who are struggling to find their footing.

In conclusion, moving forward with courage and unwavering faith means walking through life with a heart full of trust in God's plan. It means standing firm on the promises of His Word, relying on the power of the Holy Spirit, and choosing daily to live out our faith with boldness.

As we do so, we find that we are not only growing in faith ourselves but are also becoming instruments through which God's love and power can impact the world around us. May we always remember that, no matter the obstacles, we are never alone in our journey. With God by our side, we can move forward with courage, unwavering faith, and the confident assurance that He will guide us every step of the way.

FINAL THOUGHT

Unshakable faith is not a destination we arrive at, but rather an ongoing journey—one that requires intentional daily commitment and a steadfast reliance on God's goodness, power, and promises. It is not merely about reaching a point of unwavering belief, but rather about consistently choosing to trust God, especially when the circumstances of life seem overwhelming or uncertain.

In the face of trials, challenges, and unexpected obstacles, unshakable faith enables us to remain grounded, secure in the knowledge that God is faithful to His Word and will always fulfill His promises.

This journey of faith demands perseverance, as we learn to trust God not just in moments of triumph, but also in the midst of life's fiercest storms. The foundation of unshakable faith is built on the unwavering belief that God is who He says He is—our Creator, our Savior, and our constant companion. In every season, whether in times of peace or moments of hardship, we are called to stand firm in this faith, confident in the assurance that God's love never falters and His presence is always with us. Even when we cannot see the full picture, we can trust that He is guiding us, working in us, and refining our hearts to become more like Christ.

Moving forward with courage and unwavering faith requires not only trust in God's provision but also a deep confidence that He will never abandon us. His love is a constant, unshakable force that holds us steady, no matter the storms we face. Just as the apostle Paul wrote in **Romans 8:38-39 NKJV,** *"For I am persuaded that neither death nor life, nor angels nor principalities nor powers, nor things present nor things to come, nor height nor depth, nor any other created thing, shall be able to separate us from the love of God which is in Christ Jesus our Lord."* Nothing—neither hardship, nor danger, nor uncertainty—can separate us from the love of God that is in

Christ Jesus. This truth is a powerful reminder that our faith is anchored not in our own strength, but in the unfailing love of God.

As we continue this journey of faith, it is essential to stand firm in the truth that God's plans for our lives are always good, even when the path is unclear.

Jeremiah 29:11 NKJV reminds us of this comforting promise: *"For I know the thoughts that I think toward you, says the Lord, thoughts of peace and not of evil, to give you a future and a hope."* This is a promise that we can hold tightly to, knowing that no matter what comes our way, God is orchestrating every detail of our lives for His glory and our ultimate good.

In every step of our journey, we must remember that faith is not a passive act, but a powerful force that moves us to action. It is through our trust in God that we find the strength to face each day with courage and confidence. Each moment we choose to trust in Him, our faith becomes stronger and more deeply rooted in His truth. As we navigate the complexities of life, our faith serves as both our anchor and our compass, leading us toward victory and transformation.

May you be encouraged to trust God daily, knowing that His plans for you are filled with hope, purpose, and promise. May your life be a living testament to the power of unshakable faith—the kind of faith that moves mountains, overcomes obstacles, and transforms lives. As you continue to walk by faith, may you experience the joy, peace, and strength that come from trusting in the One who holds your future and guides your every step.

Stand firm in your faith, hold fast to His promises, and move forward with unwavering courage, knowing that God is always with you, strengthening your faith and empowering you to live victoriously. This journey of faith is one that leads to greater intimacy with God, greater impact on those around you, and a life that brings glory to His name.

CLOSING PRAYER: STANDING FIRM IN THE POWER OF UNSHAKABLE FAITH

Heavenly Father,

We come before You today with hearts overflowing with gratitude for the unshakable faith You have planted within us. Thank You for the incredible journey of growth and trust that we have experienced, as You have taught us to rely on Your strength and promises. Lord, as we reach the end of this chapter in our lives, we confidently declare that we will continue to stand firm in the power of faith, unwavering in our trust in You.

Your Word speaks to our hearts in **1 Corinthians 16:13 NKJV**, saying, *"Watch, stand fast in the faith, be brave, be strong."* Father, we recognize that life is full of challenges, trials, and moments of uncertainty, yet You have promised to be with us in every situation. In times of doubt and fear, help us to remember that Your strength is made perfect in our weakness (**2 Corinthians 12:9 NKJV**). We do not stand in our own power, but in the might of Your Spirit, confident that we are more than conquerors through Him who loves us (**Romans 8:37 NKJV**).

We declare with certainty that nothing will shake our faith. No matter the storms that come our way, we will stand firm on the solid foundation of Your truth. As You remind us in **Isaiah 41:10 NKJV**, *"Fear not, for I am with you; Be not dismayed, for I am your God. I will strengthen you, Yes, I will help you, I will uphold you with My righteous right hand."* Thank You, Lord, for Your faithfulness and for holding us securely in Your hands. We take great comfort in knowing that You will never leave us, and we will never be abandoned in the face of adversity.

As we continue walking this journey of faith, we commit to walking by faith and not by sight, trusting in Your guidance, even when the path ahead seems unclear (**2 Corinthians 5:7 NKJV**). We acknowledge that, though we may not always understand the twists and turns of life, You are working all things for our good and Your glory. We hold fast to Your promise that no weapon formed against us will prosper (**Isaiah 54:17 NKJV**), and we trust that You are always at work in our lives. Help us to persevere, to remain steadfast in the face of difficulties, and to always lean on Your unfailing love.

Lord, may our faith be like the tree planted by streams of water, constantly nourished and growing, bearing fruit in every season. Even amidst the winds of adversity, may we remain firmly rooted in Your Word and in the knowledge of Your faithfulness (**Psalm 1:3 NKJV**). Help us to keep our eyes fixed on Jesus, the author and perfecter of our faith, and may we follow

His example in all that we do (**Hebrews 12:2 NKJV**). In all circumstances, may we embody the same courage, humility, and grace that He demonstrated, knowing that He is our strength and our guide.

Father, we pray that our faith will continue to grow stronger with each passing day. May we be living examples of Your love, power, and grace to those around us. As we stand firm in the power of faith, may others see the hope and strength we find in You, and may they be drawn to the same unwavering trust that we have in Christ. Let our lives be a testimony to Your goodness, that all may see and glorify Your name.

We thank You for the victories, breakthroughs, and miracles that are unfolding and will continue to unfold as we stand firm in You. We thank You for Your promises, which are always true and sure, and we commit to trusting You with all our hearts. We trust that You are at work in our lives and that Your plans for us are filled with hope and purpose.

In **Philippians 4:13 NKJV,** Your Word declares, *"I can do all things through Christ who strengthens me."* We cling to this promise today, knowing that through Your strength, we can face anything that comes our way. And in **Romans 15:13 NKJV,** You offer the assurance that *"Now may the God of hope fill you with all joy and peace in believing, that you may abound in hope by the power of the Holy Spirit."* We receive this promise and stand firm in the power of Your faithfulness.

Thank You, Lord, for walking with us every step of the way. We trust You completely, knowing that in every moment, You are faithful, and You are leading us toward victory.

In the powerful name of Jesus, we pray.

Amen.

A PRAYER OF SALVATION

Heavenly Father,

I come before You today with a heart that is open and seeking. I acknowledge that I am a sinner in need of Your grace and mercy. I confess that I have fallen short of Your glory and that I cannot save myself. But I believe in Your great love for me, a love so profound that You sent Your only Son, Jesus Christ, to die on the cross for my sins and to rise again, defeating death so that I might have eternal life.

Lord Jesus, I accept You now as my Lord and Savior. I believe that You are the Son of God, that You bore my sins on the cross, and that through Your sacrifice, I am forgiven and made new. I repent of my sins, turning away from my old ways, and I invite You into my heart to transform me from the inside out.

Fill me with Your Holy Spirit, Lord, so that I may live a life that honors You. Guide me in Your truth, strengthen my faith, and help me to walk in obedience to Your Word. Teach me to love as You love, to forgive as You forgive, and to serve as You served.

Thank You for the gift of salvation, for Your unfailing grace, and for welcoming me into Your family. I surrender my life to You, trusting You with my past, present, and future. From this moment forward, I am Yours, and I declare that You are my Lord and my Savior.

In Jesus' name, I pray.

Amen

About the Author
DR. RINA F. LUCAS

Dr. Rina F. Lucas is an ordained minister, a devoted educator with over 25 years of experience, and a woman of unwavering faith. Holding two master's degrees and a doctoral degree in special education and educational leadership, she exemplifies a deep commitment to both personal and professional growth. Her passion for empowering students of all abilities reflects her belief in the transformative power of education, faith, and perseverance. She has dedicated her life to uplifting others—both in the classroom and through her ministry—by fostering hope, knowledge, and spiritual strength.

She co-founded *The Healing Ministry of Jesus Christ Church Inc.* in the Philippines, which she established alongside her father on July 4, 2019. For Dr. Lucas, this ministry is more than an institution—it fulfils God's calling to share His word, touch lives, and heal those in need. Her journey into ministry was not merely a decision but a divine assignment that she embraced with unwavering faith and obedience.

A pivotal moment in her spiritual path came through her daughter, Edrianne Mae. In March 2018, Edrianne created her first painting. When

Dr. Lucas first saw it, she believed it depicted a castle. However, Edrianne gently corrected her, saying, *"No, Mommy, this is not a castle. This is a church, and one day, you will build a church."* Those words, spoken with a childlike innocence yet divine clarity, became an undeniable confirmation of God's plan for her life. Dr. Lucas carried this vision in her heart from that moment forward, trusting that the Lord would guide her every step.

Despite the challenges of building a ministry, Dr. Lucas has remained steadfast in her faith, believing that God will provide the land, the resources, and the people needed to establish a physical church. Her dedication is fueled by an unshakable trust in God's promises, knowing He will make a way where there seems to be none. She continues to inspire, uplift, and lead others toward their spiritual breakthroughs through her work as an educator and a minister.

She sees this book as more than just a written work—it is a vessel, a testament of faith, and a step toward fulfilling God's vision in her heart. Every page reflects her journey of obedience, resilience, and unwavering trust in the Lord's divine timing.

To God be all the honor and glory, now and forever. In Jesus' name, Amen.